A Yellow Watermelon

A Yellow Watermelon

A NOVEL BY

TED M. DUNAGAN

Junebug Books

Montgomery Louisville

Junebug Books
P.O. Box 1588
Montgomery, AL 36102

Library of Congress Cataloging-in-Publication Data

Dunagan, Ted.
A yellow watermelon : a novel / by Ted Dunagan.
p. cm.
Summary: Growing up in poverty-stricken, racially segregated, rural
Alabama in the late 1940s, a white boy named Ted and a black boy
named Poudlum become secret friends, join forces to integrate the
cotton field laborers, and try to stop evil forces from depriving Poudlum's family of their property and livelihood.

ISBN-13: 978-1-58838-197-2
ISBN-10: 1-58838-197-8

[1. Race relations—Fiction. 2. Segregation—Fiction. 3. African
Americans—Fiction. 4. Prejudices—Fiction. 5. Poor—Fiction. 6.
Alabama—History—1819-1950—Fiction.] I. Title.
PZ7.D8939Ye 2007
[Fic]—dc22

2007039151

"The Setting" illustration by Linda Aldridge

Design by Randall Williams
Printed in the United States of America

To Poudlum,
MY GOOD FRIEND WHO KNEW A GOOD MELON
WHEN HE SAW ONE.

Contents

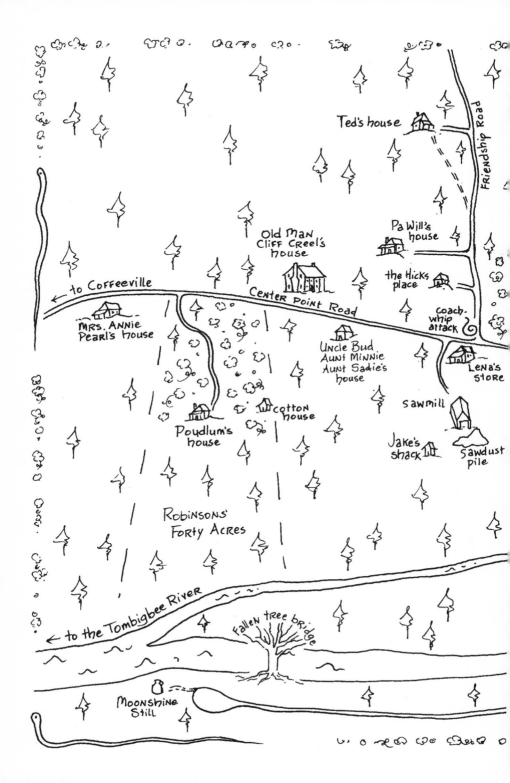

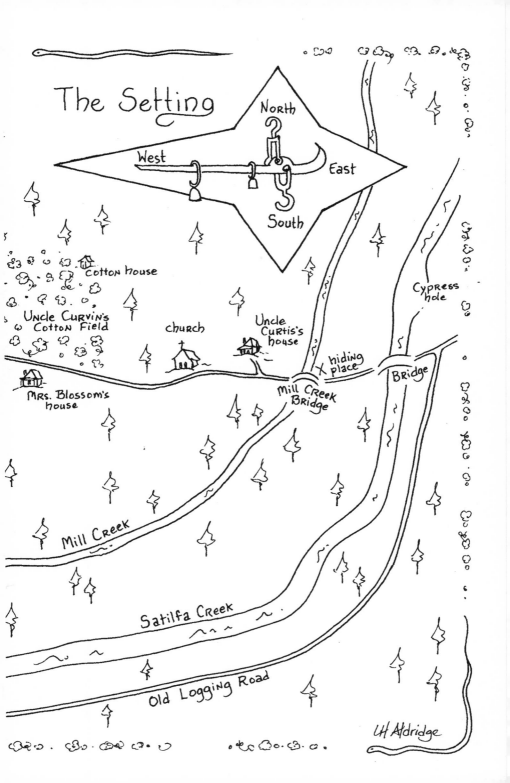

1

The Sawmill

I was forbidden to play at the sawmill, but from behind Miss Lena's store where I was nibbling on a chocolate-covered MoonPie and sipping on a peach Nehi, it beckoned to me through the shimmering heat waves.

The store was located where Friendship Road reached a dead-end at Center Point Road. There were no signs; I just knew that was what everyone called those dirt roads. The big log trucks would come roaring up from all three directions, spreading a thick layer of red dust on the roadside vegetation; then they would turn in beside Miss Lena's store to deposit their loads of logs thunderously at the sawmill behind the store.

I was turning twelve years old that late summer of 1948, savoring my last days of freedom before I had to start back to school in the fall. School was like being in prison while being forced to learn things, not to mention that you had to be scrubbed clean and wear a shirt and shoes. I spent a lot of time that summer trying to figure out a way to avoid having to go back.

The steady droning of the great saw blades began to abate and I knew it was noon. It was also Saturday, and I knew the sawmill would be deserted soon because the men, including my father, would collect their pay envelopes and go directly to Miss Lena's store for groceries or to the bootlegger for whiskey. My father usually went for groceries, but sometimes he drank whiskey.

My job wasn't finished yet, though. I had seven more *Grit* papers to sell. I remember being so excited back when I received my first fifteen papers along with a canvas bag to carry them. Also, there came a thin folding envelope with slots to place dimes, nickels, and pennies into before mailing them back. The paper sold for a nickel. I returned three pennies and kept two for each paper I sold. With a complete sell-out I made thirty cents, which seemed like a fortune. The catch was that I had to mail in forty-five cents each week whether I sold the papers or not. So far, I had never been stuck with more than two papers. On those occasions, I usually gave one to my grandfather Murphy and one to my mother.

Today hadn't been a good day. Two of my customers hadn't been home and two others just didn't have a nickel to spare. I had seven papers left and three more stops to make. The sawmill had grown quiet, like a giant beast taking a nap. I drained my Nehi and took one last look toward the mill's mountainous pile of sawdust and knew I would be back before the day was over.

Before beginning my last five-mile trek, I ventured around to the front of Miss Lena's store in the hopes of selling a paper to one of the sawmill workers. The only one I had any luck with was my father, who, after peeking inside my bag, flipped me a nickel and took a paper. I was glad to see the big bag of groceries in his other arm. He admonished me to watch out for snakes and to hurry home. I watched him walk away in his sweat-soaked shirt and pants and sawdust-covered brogans and decided I didn't want to be a sawmill worker, but I did like to play at it. I watched his big broad back disappear around the corner of Friendship Road, walking toward home; then I headed east on Center Point Road seeking my fortune.

BY THE TIME I reached the Mill Creek bridge, I was hot, thirsty, and my bare feet were burning from the sun-baked clay road. Off the road, down the bank, and underneath the wooden bridge, I stretched out on a big flat rock at the water's edge and drank my fill of the clean, cool running water before I sat up and submerged my feet. The taste and feel of the water quenched my entrepreneurial spirit and I decided to quit for the day. I had never gone home with six papers before, but I did have the money Mrs. Blossom had given me.

Mrs. Blossom was the first customer on my route each Saturday morning and she always bought a paper. Her husband ran the sawmill and they lived about a hundred yards from Miss Lena's store. After pulling the *Grit* papers out of our mailbox this morning I had inserted them into my bag and walked directly across the road to her house. Once I was on the front porch, I knocked and, as usual, yelled through the screen door, "I got your *Grit* paper here, Mrs. Blossom."

To my surprise, rather than appearing at the door with my nickel, she yelled back, "Come on in—I'm back in the kitchen."

I opened the old squeaky screen door and walked through the living room into the kitchen. To my amazement, she was sitting with great piles of money spread all over the table. There were paper dollar bills and a stack of coins in each pile. It was more money than I could imagine. She noticed the wideness of my eyes and said, "That's the payroll for the sawmill workers. Did you have breakfast this morning, Ted?"

"Yes, ma'am," I replied.

"What did you have?"

"A biscuit with fig preserves."

"Well, I'm sure you have room for a little more," she said as she pulled out a chair from the table. "Sit down here and eat this fried chicken leg. Mr. Blossom loves fried chicken for breakfast, but he wasn't too hungry this morning."

Hungry or not, I would never turn down a piece of fried chicken. Mrs. Blossom chattered away while I was eating. When I finished she handed me a rag to wipe my greasy fingers and mouth, then she placed a stack of envelopes on the table and said, "I have a job for you, Ted. There's thirteen envelopes there. I want you to stuff each one with a separate stack of money, lick it and seal it, but before you do, take yourself one nickel out of each stack."

I had wondered why there were thirteen envelopes because as far as I knew only twelve men worked at the sawmill. Now, as I sat on the rock under the Mill Creek bridge counting my money, I also wondered why Mrs. Blossom had been so generous to me. I was to find the answer to both of my questions later that day at the sawmill.

STARING AT THE NEAT STACKS of pennies, nickels, and dimes next to me on the rock, I realized it was the most money I had ever had. There were fifteen pennies, three dimes, and fourteen nickels—a dollar and fifteen cents. I reached inside my canvas bag and retrieved the return envelope and carefully inserted the forty-five cents I owed for the papers, using the pennies and dimes because they were the smallest and stood a better chance of getting lost if I kept them. Then I carefully inserted my fourteen nickels in the watch pocket of my worn mail-order jeans from Sears and Roebuck. I was having one more drink of the clear, cool water from the creek when I heard a car coming. I quickly sat back up on the rock, tilted my head back and enjoyed the eerie feeling as I watched and listened to the big heavy wooden boards of the bridge move, creak, and rumble when the car crossed over my head. While waiting for the dust to settle I gave my feet one last soaking before leaving my cool sanctuary, knowing that if I didn't dally I could be back down the road and at the sawmill in about half an hour.

A few minutes later I passed the road which led to my Uncle Curtis's house. I was tempted to stop, but the lure of the sawmill was too strong. Up the hill and around the bend I passed the Center Point Baptist Church and dreaded that tomorrow morning I would be suffering inside it. It would be extremely hot and the only relief would come from a cardboard fan with a wooden handle like a big Popsicle stick d a picture of Jesus on it. Before the service, the women would congregate in the churchyard and talk about their vegetable gardens, their chickens, the price of sugar and flour, and dozens of other subjects of no interest to me. The men would talk about the price of timber and the crops in the fields. My father never went to church; in fact the only time I ever remember seeing him in that church was years later at his funeral, and of course he wouldn't have been there then if it had been up to him. Tomorrow morning while I was sitting in there sweating, he would probably be sitting in a cool hollow in the woods hunting wild turkeys.

The service would officially get under way when Addie Brooks, without any sheet music, started playing the old upright piano and everyone stood and began singing, "Shall We Gather At The River." As soon as the haunting notes of the hymn faded away, the collection plate would be passed and my mother would watch me closely to make sure I put in one of my hard-earned nickels. Then the preacher would start ranting and raving and praying for what seemed like an eternity. I would be praying too—for him to please shut up so I could get out of there and get out back to the pump for a cool drink of water.

But that was tomorrow; today I was heading for the sawmill. Before I got there I passed the cotton field of my Uncle Curvin, Uncle Curtis's twin brother. The plants were taller than me and turning brown. The hard green bolls were beginning to burst open. In a week or so I would be out there pulling the fluffy white fibers out of their prickly bolls. Uncle Curvin had promised me last year that I would be big enough to pick this year. He paid a penny a pound. I would be out there making a lot of money real soon.

MISS LENA'S STORE came into view and I slowed to time my prohibited entrance into the sawmill. I passed Mrs. Blossom's house and the store, looked up and down the road to make sure it was deserted, and darted into the woods. After a short distance I doubled back and came out of the woods in the area where the logs were unloaded from the trucks. There, behind a huge mound of pine logs, I was hidden from view. On the ground in front of me was a peavey, a big wooden lever with a metal point and a hinged metal hook near the end. The men used this tool to handle the logs. I reached down and grasped the big round hickory handle and lifted it off the ground while I contemplated moving one of the great logs. When I felt the full weight of the peavey and studied the jumbled pile of timber, I dismissed the idea, knowing I could get crushed like a bug if the logs started rolling.

Not so with the neat stacks of lumber. I could climb up the back side and peek over the tops toward the road. I tried this on several stacks wishing I could stand on top and see how far I could see, but daring not for fear of being spotted from the road. The stacks were different every week, in size and types of cuts, because trucks came on Mondays to haul the rough-sawn lumber away to another mill where it was planed smooth into a finished product.

After exploring each stack of lumber I entered into the bowels of the beast, past the motor and the conveyor belts, to the great round saw blade which they turned. I climbed down into the pit which housed the part of the saw which was below ground level and stood face to face with it. I reached out and touched the smooth shiny steel and pressed my fingertip against one of the sharp teeth and imagined how the giant blade would look and sound turning at full speed with me standing there next to it. That was enough to get me out of that pit.

Next, I ventured down the long wooden ramp where the slabs were disposed of. These were the irregular parts with bark on them which were cut away from the outer portion of the logs before they were sawn into lumber. The ramp had side rails about chest high to a grown man, and the rail tops were worn smooth as a kitten's fur from the constant wear of the slabs being laid across them and pushed off the end of the ramp into the fire pit below.

The fire never went out. It blazed high all day and turned into a huge bed of coals at night and on weekends.

I stretched out on my belly, hung my head over the edge of the ramp, gazed down and wondered if the inferno below was anything like the burning hell the preacher was always yelling about. Feeling the heat blistering my face, I scooted backwards on the rough boards to a safe distance from the edge, got to my feet, and headed for my favorite spot—the monstrous sawdust pile.

When the sawmill was operating, a conveyor belt carried the sawdust away from the mill and dumped it on the top of the mound, where it cascaded down in all directions. That's what I wanted to do, slide down that sawdust pile.

On many occasions I had been told to stay off the pile because it might cave in, suck me under, and I would smother or burn up because there was a fire inside it. But I knew those were just tales everyone told to scare me away from the sawmill.

At the base of the sawdust mountain, I found a scrap

board on which I carefully stacked my eleven nickels and laid my canvas bag. I knew that if my money fell out of my pocket during a slide it would be lost forever.

Climbing up was difficult. My bare feet sank past my ankles while I clawed upward with my hands. I stopped midway up, looked down and thought about sliding back to the bottom from there. But I decided to struggle on to the top for the ultimate thrill of sliding all the way down.

When I arrived at the summit, just as I had from the lumber stacks, I peeked over and surveyed the road, the store, and Mrs. Blossom's house. There were no sounds or movement anywhere. Everything seemed frozen in the heat of the day.

Turning, I gazed downward and started running to get a good start. It was like running in slow motion. After several steps, I threw my feet into the air, landed on my seat, and watched the world go racing by.

After a soft landing—covered with sawdust from head to toe—I climbed back up and checked out the world around me again.

Everything still looked the same, but just to be safe I carefully looked all around the sawmill knowing someone could have come through the woods just as I had, see me, tell on me, and eventually I would be feeling the sting of a long switch from a peach tree.

The only thing that bothered me was that the door to the old black tar-papered shack off to the right was open. Was it open before? I couldn't remember, but somehow it bothered me.

I decided that after this slide I should vacate the sawmill

area, but I wanted to make it a good one, so I moved a quarter of the way around the mountain to smooth sawdust. The move took me out of the sight of my belongings below.

Once again, the world sped by while I surfed the sawdust all the way to the bottom. Again, I was completely covered with it. I slipped out of my jeans and t-shirt, shook them vigorously, quickly put them back on, and walked around the sawdust pile to retrieve my money and *Grit* bag. But when I arrived where I had left them, I stood there stunned. I couldn't believe it. They were both gone!

2

Jake

Standing there staring at that empty piece of scrap lumber realizing that my little fortune, as well as my prized canvas bag containing the envelope with the forty-five cents I owed the *Grit* paper were gone, I silently began to cry. I thought I felt the worst I had ever felt in my young life; that is until I heard the deep gruff voice behind me ask, "What's yo' name, boy?"

I started to run, but I was just too scared. Slowly, I turned to face the voice and there stood the blackest man I had ever seen. He was well over six feet tall and needed a shave, but was handsome even in his overalls and sweat-stained work shirt. Most importantly, and much to my relief, he was grinning. It was a friendly disarming grin which gave flight to my fear.

"Cat got yo' tongue, boy?"

"Uh, no sir."

"Den what's yo' name?"

"Uh, Ted. Ted Dillon, sir."

"You one of Mister J. D.'s boys?"

"Yes, sir."

"You can forget dat 'sir' business. You don't wants no white folks hearing you 'sir-ing' a black man. You gots some brothers, too, don't you?"

I wasn't afraid anymore and I knew he was correct, that I would be called down hard if I was to be heard calling him "sir." "Yeah, I got two brothers," I answered.

"What's dey names?"

"My oldest brother is Ned, then Fred, then me."

"And you Ted. My, my. Why you think yo' momma named y'all all dem rhyming names?"

"I don't know. Guess they were the only ones she could think of."

"No, I 'spect maybe she a poet. You needs to learn to look at things a little harder and think a little deeper. Things ain't always what dey seems to be on the surface."

I knew I needed to think about that a while, so I just said, "Uh, okay."

"And you can be proud to have Mister J. D. for yo' daddy. He a good man. I sho wouldn't want to get into no scuffle wid him. He know you messing around dis here sawmill?"

"No. You gonna tell on me?"

"I don't know. I gots to think on it a while."

At that I figured I might as well cut a switch on the way home, because come late Monday when my father came home from work and told my mother, she would be using it on me. I guess my new acquaintance saw the look on my face and felt sorry for me because he said, "We might be able to work something out, Ted. By de way, my name is Jake."

I reached out and shook his big rough hand and asked, "What do you mean?"

"I mean if you make me a promise, I might forget about yo' visit today."

I asked cautiously, "What do I have to promise?"

"Dat you won't play around dis sawmill by yoself no mo. It's a dangerous place. Why, a log could roll on you, and what if you had slipped up on dat slab ramp and fell in dat fire pit? You would've been fried crisper dan a piece of fatback. Now, if you'll make me dat promise, I won't ever tell a soul about you being here today. How 'bout it?"

I had to think about this. I could take a switching, but I couldn't give up the sawmill forever. I decided to see if he would compromise. "Could I still just slide down the sawdust pile?"

"Only if someone else is wid you, including me."

I figured that was the best I could get so I said, "It's a deal. I promise."

"Dat's a good boy. Come on over here by my fire and let's talk for a few minutes."

I followed him over to beside the tar paper shack where he had a big bed of hot coals he had shoveled from the fire pit. A coffee pot was bubbling away. I watched as he picked up a blue tin cup off the ground and pulled a big red handkerchief from his pocket which he used as a hot pad to pour his coffee. Then he sat on a block of wood and said, "Ted, besides promising to stay away from de dangers of dis sawmill, I think you learned another lesson today."

Only then did I remember my money and my bag. I knew he must have taken them, but I wasn't quite sure yet if I should ask him, so I just said, "What other lesson?"

"De lesson dat you should never leave valuables unattended. You agree wid dat?"

"Uh huh," I answered while nodding my head. He reached behind his seat and retrieved my money and bag, handed them both to me, and asked, "Did you make all dat money selling dem little papers?"

"Not all of it. Mrs. Blossom gave me thirteen of the nickels."

"Why did Mrs. Blossom give you so much money?"

I told him the story about the pay envelopes and he asked, "Did she ever do dat before?"

"No. Never did."

"I reckon she just feeling sorry for you."

"What for?"

"Can you keep a secret? Remember, I'm keeping yours."

I had counted my nickels and was redepositing them into my watch pocket when I answered, "Yeah, I sure can."

"She was feeling sorry for you because yo' daddy is gon' lose his job soon."

This was bad news because I could remember my father being out of work before and I knew how we had suffered. I thought about it for a few moments and then asked, "Why would my daddy lose his job? He works real hard."

"He does dat, but dat's not the problem. The problem is dat Mr. Blossom is gonna shut dis sawmill down and move to Mobile and go into de wholesale lumber business."

"How you know?"

"'Cause I work for Mr. Blossom and he told me."

"You work here at the sawmill too?"

"Yep, started dis week."

Now I knew why there were thirteen pay envelopes this morning, but my curiosity prompted more questions. "Where do you live?"

"Right here, in dis old tar paper shack."

"I thought that's where they keep the drums of fuel to run the sawmill?"

"It is, but I rearranged dem and made room for a cot Mrs. Blossom gave me. I does my cooking right here. I never run out of hot coals."

"How did you come to work for Mr. Blossom?"

"I was working east of here, over in Greensboro at de planing mill and I ran into him. He told me about dis job and since I'm working my way west, I just rode over here wid him."

"How far west you going, Mississippi?"

"Shoot, boy, it's just a few miles to de Mississippi state line. I'm going a lot farther dan dat. I'm going all de way to California!"

That sounded faraway to me since I had never been farther than twenty miles away from home. My brothers told me we had traveled all the way down to Mobile once, but I had been too little to remember. They also told me our father had worked there building ships during the world war, but I only remembered him sharecropping some land and working off and on at the sawmill.

Jake broke my train of thought when he asked, "How old is you?"

"I'm almost twelve."

"'Spect you'll be going back to school dis fall?"

"I guess so, unless I can figure a way out of it."

"Hey, you listens and listens to me good. You go to school as long as you possibly can, den go some more."

"How come Mr. Blossom's going to close the sawmill?"

"He says he ain't making no money 'cause de cost of fuel has gone up. I think it's really because Mrs. Blossom don't like living out here in de middle of nowhere, but it ain't really none of my concern."

"When's he gonna close it?"

"In a few weeks."

This was more bad news. That would be just about the time my mother would need money to order us shoes and clothes for school and the winter. And where would we get the money to buy lunch at school? On school days she gave each of us fifteen cents every morning for our lunch. I started trying to figure out how much that would be a week for all three of us.

Jake interrupted my ciphering when he said, "Don't you be worrying yo' young head about dis old sawmill shutting down. Yo' daddy will find something to do. Say, you want to sell one of dem *Grit* papers, or do you already have dem sold?"

My spirits leaped. I was going to make another nickel. "No, I got six of them left," I said as I eagerly reached into my bag.

I watched as he pulled a leather purse with metal clasps from the bib pocket of his overalls and open it, then I was stunned when he said, "I'll take all six of 'em."

I stared at him for a moment before I asked, "What for? They all say the same thing."

"Oh, I'll read one of dem, and den I'll have another use for it, along with the others."

I didn't ask any questions. I just handed him the papers, accepted the quarter and the nickel he gave me, and placed them into my watch pocket along with the rest of my fortune, totaling eighty-five cents.

I glanced at the sun and knew I should be heading toward home because it was already close to supper time, but I had decided I liked Jake and I wanted to talk to him some more. So I asked, "What do you do here by yourself?"

"I read books, tell stories, play cards, and pick my guitar."

"Who do you tell stories to?"

"Myself."

"Who do you play cards with?"

"Myself."

"Will you teach me how to play cards?"

"No way. Yo' momma would skin me alive. But I will tell you some stories. Not today though. It's getting late and you ought to be heading home."

"I guess you'll be heading west when the sawmill closes?"

"Not right away. Mr. Blossom's gon' pay me to stay until all de parts are sold and moved away. By den I'll have me a pretty good stake, den I'll head west."

"Well, I guess I better get going. Can I bring you a *Grit* paper next Saturday?"

"You sho can. And you can stop by here anytime you're

around after everything has shut down for de day. I'll tell you some good stories."

I got up from the ground where I had been sitting, brushed off the seat of my pants and said, "I'm glad I met you, Jake, and thank you for buying my papers."

"I'm glad we met, too, Ted. Remember to keep our secret 'cause it won't do no good for nobody to know about dis old sawmill closing. Now you just walk straight up to de road instead of sneaking through dem woods. If anybody sees you, we'll just say you came and sold me a *Grit* paper, which is de truth."

I didn't know what else to say so I just walked away, straight up to Miss Lena's store where I spent a nickel and bought ten peanut butter logs. They were small sticks of candy with a thin coat of peppermint on the outside and peanut butter in the inside, sealed in clear cellophane paper. I ate two and stored the others in my canvas bag.

JUST BEFORE I TURNED onto Friendship Road toward home I stopped for one last look down toward the sawmill and saw Jake with a big shovel transferring more hot coals to his fire. I supposed he was getting ready to cook his supper and I felt bad knowing he had to eat alone, but there was nothing I could do, so I turned the corner walking toward home.

It wasn't far to the first house where Earl and Merle Hicks lived, who weren't any kin to me, but they were friends of my mother and father. I didn't see anybody stirring about so I kept walking. Just past their house was the road to my grandfather Murphy's house, which was farther off the road than the Hicks'. I looked down the little road and I could see him sitting in his rocking chair on the front porch. I wished I had saved a paper for him. I made a resolution not to be so selfish next Saturday and save one for him. I knew his poor vision prevented him from seeing me, and it wasn't long before sundown, so I walked on.

There were no more houses between there and home, just that old dirt road with thick woods hanging over it from each side, but it was only about a mile farther.

While I was walking that mile I started thinking about Jake. He had told me where he was going, but not where he came from. I decided I would have to ask him about that sometime soon. Those faraway places he talked about made me feel very small and isolated. I knew we lived in the lower part of Alabama close to the Mississippi state line. I also knew we lived in Clarke County and that Grove Hill was the county seat, twenty miles east, and I had been there a few times.

I had been to Coffeeville many times, which was only nine miles from Miss Lena's store, straight on out Center Point Road which turned from dirt road into blacktop just before you got into town—that is if you wanted to call it a town. There was a store which was a lot bigger than Miss Lena's, a gas station, a feed and seed store, and a cafe with no name.

That was about it, except, oh yes, there was the big red brick school house where I was soon to be incarcerated. And I almost forgot, there was also the river at Coffeeville, the Tombigbee. It was a big old river, deep, wide, and muddy. On a foggy morning you couldn't see across it. Sometimes we ate fried catfish my father caught out of it.

When I reached the top of the big hill I noticed the sky had gotten darker, but I knew there was an hour or so of daylight left. Looking toward the west I saw a dark gathering of clouds and knew there were thunderstorms on the way. I quickened my step, descended down the big hill, and didn't stop until I reached the top of the little hill. I had a decision to make there. I could turn off the road and take the trail through the woods, which was a shortcut to my house, or I could stay on the open road and take the long way home. I decided on the latter since the shadows were beginning to lengthen. Besides, sometimes my brother Fred hid on the trail and tried to scare me.

When I turned off Friendship Road onto the sandy road leading toward home, I could smell supper and it reminded me how hungry I was. The first thing I saw was my oldest brother Ned carrying a big armload of stove wood toward the back door. I knew something was wrong. Ned's job was to saw and split the slabs from the sawmill into small sticks which would fit into the wood-burning kitchen stove, and it was Fred's job to carry it in.

Then I saw my mother standing on the front porch brandishing a long switch from one of her peach trees, and my heart sank. Someone must have seen me at the sawmill after all.

3

Dinner on the Grounds

It turned out that the switch was meant for my brother Fred, who didn't show up to do his assigned chores. I figured this out when I approached the front porch expecting to feel the sting of the switch and heard my mother ask, "Do you know where your brother Fred is?"

"No ma'am," I answered while washing my hands. Afterwards I headed for the kitchen where I knew supper awaited me. Our three meals were breakfast, dinner at midday, and supper at night. There on the big black wood stove was my supper. On one of the eyes, still warm, was a big pot of fresh black-eyed peas with tiny pods of boiled okra floating on top. On the apron of the stove was a bowl of creamed corn, a bowl of chopped fried okra, and a plate of sliced ruby-red tomatoes—all fresh that day from my mother's garden. The crispy brown cornbread was sliced and still in the black skillet. I piled my plate high, ate my fill, and washed it down with a big glass of buttermilk.

Afterwards, I walked from the kitchen through the main

room, by my mother and father's bed, the fireplace, and the two big rocking chairs. My parents were on the front porch, where in the fading light, she was shelling butter beans and he was cleaning his old shotgun.

At the end of the porch was the door which led into the room—built like an afterthought onto the side of the old shack—where my brothers and I slept.

THE STORM CAME LATER than I expected. When the hard rain hit the old tin roof it jarred me from a deep sleep. You would have had to shout to make someone hear you over the explosive noise, but I wasn't afraid because I had heard it many times before. After a while the rain subsided into a soft, hypnotic patter on the tin. Just before it soothed me back to sleep, I ran my hand over the rough sheet which my mother made by sewing empty flour sacks together, to find that Fred wasn't in his accustomed place. A little later on, I felt the dampness of him as he slid into bed.

I woke up to the smell of fried chicken. I sat up in bed thinking this must be a special day if we're having fried chicken for breakfast. Seeing the room was empty, I leapt out of bed, hoping my older brothers hadn't eaten both the drumsticks.

On the front porch, because I knew I would be asked when I arrived in the kitchen, I stopped and washed my hands. The drinking bucket and wash basin sat on a bench at the end of the porch. I took the dipper from a nail on the wall, splashed water into the basin, and scrubbed my hands good with the big brown bar of soap. Afterwards, I threw the soapy water out into the yard and dried my hands on the thin towel hanging on another nail next to the dipper. There was no running water, and there was no indoor plumbing. We had to carry our drinking water in buckets from a well we shared with the Bedwell family. Water for bathing and washing clothes was collected in a big rain barrel at the rear of the house underneath a low spot on the roof. I knew it would be full after last night's storm.

When I arrived in the kitchen, I was surprised to find no one there except my mother. "Where is everybody?" I asked.

"Your daddy and Ned have already gone to the woods to hunt. Fred is behind the house getting a bath. I told him to save his tub of water for you. Now, sit down and eat your breakfast," she said, placing a plate in front of me with a fried egg and a hot biscuit. Then she slid a mason jar of her homemade blackberry jam toward me.

I glanced at my food, then stared at the big platter of fried chicken at the other end of the table. She followed my gaze and said, "You can have all the chicken you want after church. We're having dinner-on-the-grounds right after the service."

My heart leapt. This meant all kinds of delicious food would be stacked high on the wooden tables lined up in the shade of the big oak trees beside the church. We would probably even get out early.

While sopping up the last of the egg yoke and jam with the remains of my biscuit, I found myself wondering what Jake was having for breakfast, if anything. Jake was the first black person I had seen up close and talked to, though I had observed them from a distance. Most recently was in the early summer at my Uncle Curvin's cotton field where a group of black workers—hoes in hand—were climbing down from the back of his pickup. It had been the time of year when the cotton had to be chopped with a hoe to thin out the overcrowded plants and eliminate the weeds.

I had come along as the water boy, and later in the day, when the heat became intense, I would walk down the long, straight rows with a bucket of water and a dipper so the white people could have a cool drink. I remembered looking across the field, where on the other side, a black boy who looked about my size and age was doing the same for the black people. In 1948, even the cotton fields in lower Alabama were segregated.

My thoughts were interrupted when my mother said, "Fred ought to be finished by now. Go on out and get your bath and I'll have your Sunday clothes ready when you get back."

When I walked around the corner of the house I saw my brother standing naked on a board beside the galvanized wash tub which he had filled from the rain barrel. He had just finished drying off and was stepping into his jeans. I noticed there were no red marks on his legs or back and asked, "You didn't get a switching for being late?"

"Naw. I was over at Uncle Clyde's house. The storm came early over there and I had to wait until it was over before I could come home."

I stripped, stepped into the tub, and sat down in the cool soapy water. Just before Fred disappeared around the corner he said, "By the way, I peed in the tub."

"Mother!" I yelled.

He was back in a flash saying, "Shut up! I was just kidding with you. Okay?"

My brother, I thought, was itching to get a whipping. I figured he timed that storm just right so he could be late and get away with it. I also knew he had been fighting his Bantam rooster for money, and that he shot marbles for keeps. My mother considered both of those as gambling, but I kept his secrets. I had a lot of secrets.

On the way to church, Fred and I sat on the tailgate of Uncle Curtis's pickup, letting our feet drag along the dirt road. I had on last year's shoes which were too small and hurt my feet, but I knew I had to suffer until church was over. Last night's rain had settled the dust so I didn't have to worry about it soiling my one white shirt, which my mother had starched and pressed to perfection with her heavy black iron, heated on her kitchen stove.

When we turned the corner onto Center Point Road, I looked toward the sawmill, thought about Jake and asked Fred, "You ever talk to a black person?"

"We ain't supposed to talk to niggers, unless we telling them what to do. Why?"

"I just wondered." I had suspected this was how everyone felt. Now that it was confirmed, I decided I couldn't share my encounter with Jake, even with my brother.

Everyone parked their vehicles in the shade of the oak trees next to the church and left the food inside them. When we arrived I was amazed to see my mother get out of the cab of the pickup, Fred jump inside in her place, and roar away with my cousin Robert at the wheel.

"Where're they going?" I asked my mother.

"They have to go get the blocks of ice and chip it up for the iced tea."

I was left to suffer alone. The worst part started immediately. It was the hugging, kissing, and pinching by all my aunts and great-aunts. I could close my eyes and know which one it was just by their smells. My father's sister, Aunt Cleo, always smelled sweet like wild flowers; in fact, today she had a bouquet of daisies pined to the bodice of her Sunday dress, held there by a big orange-colored cameo pin. My mother's two sisters, Aunt Allie May and Aunt Lallie Grey, smelled like her, like some wonderful smell from the kitchen. Today, it was the aroma of fresh-baked cake. There was no mistaking the two sisters of my mother's mother, Aunt Minnie and Aunt Sadie, who both smelled like peach-flavored snuff.

I felt suffocated and my face ached from having my cheeks pinched. Finally, I escaped when everyone's attention turned toward the new Chevrolet Fleetwood station wagon pulling into the churchyard. It was Old Man Cliff Creel.

That was how everyone referred to him—as Old Man Cliff Creel. He was the only rich man I knew and he seemed to own just about everything. Miss Lena's store wasn't really Miss Lena's. It belonged to Mr. Creel. As did the sawmill, the land where Uncle Curvin grew his cotton, and most of the other farm land around. Anytime anyone pointed out a field, more often than not someone would say, "Old man Cliff Creel owns that." He owned the trucks which hauled the logs and the forests where the logs were cut. He even owned the three-room shack where we lived; my father had to pay him twelve dollars a month for rent.

If anybody wanted to borrow money, then Mr. Creel was the only source, and there would be interest to pay. I had passed many times by his big white house, about a mile past Miss Lena's store heading toward Coffeeville, but had never even entered his front yard. It was just too intimidating. I had heard folks say he kept a mean dog behind the picket fence with a manicured lawn on each side of the walkway, leading up to flower beds and shrubbery in front of the long front porch, which was lined with swings and rocking chairs.

There were also several outbuildings, including a large barn and a smokehouse which was almost as big as our house. I had never seen Mr. Creel without a hat, except inside the church, and today was no exception. As soon as he got out of his new car the preacher rushed over to shake his hand and welcome him. They were the only two men there wearing suits and neckties.

Old Man Cliff Creel looked fat and mean to me. His face was shaved clean, framing his fat nose which was crisscrossed with tiny red and blue veins. I remembered my mother saying that was a sign of a man who had drunk too much whiskey for too long. Below his nose were thin lips between which I could see his tobacco-stained teeth. When he and the preacher began walking toward the front door of the church everyone knew that it was time to start. As they walked through the crowd everyone would say, "Good morning, Mister Creel."

He would nod to people while he kept walking. I saw the glint of the sun's reflection off the gold bar on his necktie when he walked by me, and I shrank away.

THE ANNOUNCEMENTS HAD been made, the hymns sung, the collection plate passed, the prayer that lasted for what seemed like eternity had been prayed, and now Brother Benny Hurd was deep into his sermon. About then I felt an itch so deep it was almost painful. It was coming from just below my waistline and I knew at once that a redbug was embedded in my skin. I gritted my teeth, thought about the wonderful food I was about to have, jumping into the cool water of Satilfa Creek, or dousing that nasty chigger with some rubbing alcohol. When I could stand it no longer I plunged my hand into my pants and began scratching vigorously; that is, until my mother started whacking my head with the edge of her Jesus fan.

I became very still until everyone's attention was back on the preacher, then I slowly turned my head toward the window. From my seat on the end of the pew I saw Fred and Robert kneeling over two wash tubs containing huge blocks of ice. They were attacking the blocks with ice picks and I could see chunks falling away from the blocks into the tubs. I saw Fred insert a sliver of ice into his mouth. He looked up, saw me, and must have felt guilty because he turned his back toward me.

A little river of sweat, starting from beside my ear, had trickled down my face onto my neck where another aggravating itch had begun, but I dared not scratch.

I didn't know how much longer I could stand it. My belly was itching, my neck was itching, I was hot, I was thirsty, and I was hungry. I decided to try to listen to the preacher and see if I could make any sense out of what he was yammering about. It was about something in the Bible where one brother killed the other. I listened while he said, "After Cain, out of jealously, killed his brother Abel, God put a mark on him and banished him to the land of Nod, east of Eden, where he would be a fugitive and vagabond for all his days on the earth."

Preacher had my attention, but I wasn't sure what he was talking about. He paused, took a handkerchief from his pocket, mopped his face, and glanced out the window toward the big oak trees. I sat up straight and thought, yes, he's thinking about iced tea and fried chicken, too.

He continued: "Yes, my friends, look around you and see who has the curse of the mark of God."

I slid up on the edge of my seat and gripped the back of the pew in front of me. I certainly wanted to know who God had cursed and what kind of mark He had put on them. In case I ran into one, I definitely wanted to recognize them. My itching, hunger, and thirst were gone as I anxiously waited for the preacher to reveal this great secret.

His voice was rising now as he abandoned the lectern and walked to the left side of the podium, directly in front of Old Man Cliff Creel. "Who among us are the vagabonds and the fugitives? Who among us bear the mark of the curse of God?"

I was beside myself, thinking, why doesn't he just tell us?

Preacher's voice was a roar now as he pumped his fist into the air. "I ask you, who among us tills the earth, but it no longer yields its strength to them? It's the black man! He wears the mark of the curse! My friends, it's the niggers!"

I was astounded as I heard Old Man Cliff Creel yell, "Amen, brother."

The sermon was concluded and Brother Benny called everyone to their feet to sing the closing hymn. Every once in a while he would break in, and as only the piano played softly, he would invite people down to the altar to be saved or rededicate their lives to Jesus.

I don't know whether it was my prayer to be released or the food outside, but no one wanted to be saved that day.

Finally, mercifully, it was over. Everyone was outside, smiling, talking and eating. I knew where the best food was. The fried chicken and the butter beans were my mother's, then I helped myself to Aunt Ola's potato salad and Aunt Lillian's banana pudding. I cleaned my plate and drained my iced tea along with Fred and Robert on the tailgate of Uncle Curtis's pickup.

Through it all I kept thinking about the end of the preacher's sermon. I had never heard of the land of Nod. I thought black people came from Africa, and I was glad they had, because somehow they had managed to bring some okra seeds with them. Without them, there would be no fried okra.

There were a lot of questions in my mind, but I knew this was not the time, the place, and there was not a person—then I thought, Jake! I had to figure out a way to get to the sawmill, today!

Almost immediately opportunity presented itself. While cleaning up my mother told me, "Go get on the truck. We're going to visit at your Uncle Curtis's for a while."

"Can I just walk on home? I want to see if Ned and Daddy are home yet. See what they got."

"Well, I suppose. You just be careful."

During the confusion of everyone packing up I snatched a chicken leg and a pulley bone, quickly wrapped them in a piece of used wax paper, and stuffed them into my pocket. Just before leaving, I took off the hurtful shoes and tossed them in the back of the truck.

4

Nail Soup

I dashed into the woods just past Miss Lena's store. When I reached the first pile of logs, not yet in sight of Jake's shack, I stopped dead in my tracks. I heard a strange, rhythmic, melodious, wonderful sound—one I had never heard before, and I liked it.

The sound stopped. I stood frozen in my spot and waited for it to start again. It didn't, so I walked on past the far end of the sawmill and there was Jake, sitting on a block of wood, staring into his bed of hot coals with his old guitar resting across his knees.

He looked up at that moment and I said, "Hello, Jake."

"Ted! Well, now, don't you look nice. You been to church?"

"Yeah, we had dinner-on-the-grounds today."

"Been a long time since I been to one of dem, but I remember all dat fine food. I was just getting ready to fry me up a couple of flapjacks. I 'spect you too full to join me."

"Yeah, I'm stuffed. But I brought you a couple of pieces of fried chicken to go with your flapjacks."

"Lawd have mercy," Jake said as he unfolded the wax

paper. "You be Mister Ted from now on. Bless yore little heart, Mister Ted. Why you do dis?"

I wanted to tell him that I had always been taught to offer a gift if you wanted something, and I did want something from him. I wanted answers, but I didn't know how to explain this, so I just said, "I don't know. Just saw all that food and thought you might like some."

"You mind if I go ahead and eat dis chicken? Dem flapjacks can wait."

"No. Go ahead."

I watched while Jake ate his chicken, threw the bones into the fire, then wiped his hands on his handkerchief. Only then did I feel it was appropriate to question him. But the questions the preacher had raised could wait, because I had to know about the music. "Jake, you were playing your guitar and singing before I got here, weren't you?"

"I sho was. You heard me?"

"I sure did."

"You like it?"

"I liked it very much, but I never heard anything like it before. What kind of music was it?"

"Why, dem wuz de blues. I wuz singing de blues."

"What in the world is the blues?"

"Well, now, dat's kinda hard to explain, but I goings to try. De blues is something deeper dan a mood. It—it comes from heartache caused by want, need, hurt, loss, hard work, sacrifices, and things like dat."

"Why would you want to sing about stuff like that?"

"You just full of questions today, and dat's another tough one. I s'pose singing de blues kind of makes dose things not seem quite so bad, plus it's a reminder that they do exist."

"Can just black folks sing the blues?"

"Shoot no. White folks can sing 'em too. I've heard 'em do it."

"Where do the songs come from?"

"I just makes 'em up as I go along."

"How in the world do you do that?"

"I be happy to show you. Dis'll be yo' song. You just pick out a subject."

"I don't know how to do that."

"Sho you do. Pick out something like being hungry with no food, some kind of hard work, or—"

"How about this old sawmill?" I interrupted.

"Oh yeah, dat's easy."

I watched while Jake started strumming on his guitar, then suddenly he picked up the pace and broke into song:

"Got dem old sawmill blues

"De kind you just can't lose

"Got sawdust in my clothes

"Got sawdust in my nose

"Sweat all in my eyes

"I ain't telling no lies

"No time to drink no booze

"'Cause I got dem old sawmill blues . . ."

I sat there on that block of wood and was completely captured by the essence of the words, the sounds of the instrument and Jake's voice. It was as if I could actually feel the music, an experience I had never had before. He went through the song four times and I had it memorized by the time he hit his last chord on his guitar. The sound and the wonder of the music lingered in my memory, and I was still tapping my toe, even after it was over.

We moved away from the heat of the sun and hot coals onto a bench in a spot of shade beside Jake's shack. The bench was simply a scrap board resting on two more blocks of wood.

We sat in silence for a few moments before Jake said, "You got something else besides de blues on yo' mind, don't you?"

"Yeah, how you know?"

"You just quiet and thoughtful looking."

I felt awkward and knew even at my young age that I was broaching a sensitive subject, but somehow I knew Jake would understand and explain things to me. I started slowly, reached a comfort level, then proceeded to tell him the entire story about the last part of the preacher's sermon.

When I finished, once again, we sat in silence for a while until Jake asked, "So what you think about what yo' preacher said?"

I had been waiting for him to tell me what he thought. Now he was asking me, so I told him. "I ain't too sure that preacher was right at all."

"You can bet yo' bottom dollar on dat. He was right by saying a mark was put on Cain and he wuz sent off to de Land of Nod. But de next time you see dat preacher, tell him to read further and de Bible will say dat Cain and his family went on to be folks who lived in tents and raised livestock. Don't sound like black folks to me. He just trying to stir up some hate. Proud to see it didn't work on you."

"You read the Bible?"

"Read it from cover to cover."

"When did you do that?"

"When I was in de— While back when I had a little time on my hands."

"How about that word, the one y'all don't like to be called?" I didn't want to say it.

"You means, *nigger*?"

"Yeah."

"What about it?'

"Where did it come from and how come y'all don't like it?"

"It come from back in the slave times when ignorant folks couldn't pronounce Negro. I s'pose we don't like it 'cause it reminds us of dat part of our past. Now, anything else bothering you today?"

Jake had awakened the music in my soul, erased the doubts in my mind, and added to my education that day. I still wasn't sure what that preacher was up to. It was as if he had been preaching to Old Man Cliff Creel. I would have to ponder on that.

In the meantime, there was one more thing bothering me about Jake. "You ain't got no garden and no chickens. You can't live on flapjacks. What else do you eat?"

"I went to Miz Miss Lena's after you left yesterday and bought myself some groceries."

"What'd you buy?"

"I got me some tins of sardines, a few cans of pork 'n beans, box of soda crackers, sack of flour, and a bucket of lard."

"My mother says you can't live on stuff like that. You

need fresh fruit and vegetables, eggs, and occasionally a piece of meat."

"She absolutely right. Eggs is what I miss most. Dey would go mighty fine with my flapjacks in the mornings. But if worst comes to worst, I can always make myself some nail soup."

"Nail soup—what in the world is that?"

"You never heard de story 'bout nail soup?"

"No, never did. Will you tell me?"

"I sho will. Can't rightly say whether I read it or somebody told it to me, but it goes like dis:

"Dey was a gentlemen traveling by foot down a lonely road. It came on toward dinner time and a powerful hunger came upon him. A little farther down de road he came up on a farm house and dey was a lady in de front yard raking leaves. He decided to ask her for some food. Stopping at the front yard gate he spoke saying, 'Top of the day to you, ma'am. I been traveling all day, I'm real hungry, and wondered if you might be able to spare a little food.'

"The woman replied, 'I'm hungry myself, but I don't have a scrap of food in the whole house.'

"De traveler said, 'Well, in dat case, maybe I can help you. Do you happen to have some water and a cooking pot?'

"'Why, yes, I do.'

"Reaching into his pocket, de traveler pulled out a shiny nail and said, 'I have a magic nail here. If we put it into a pot of boiling water it will make a fine soup, den we both can eat.'

"'Do tell,' the lady said. 'Come on in the house and let's put a pot of water on the fire.'

"Once the water was boiling the traveler dropped the nail in the pot and said, 'Now, pretty soon we'll have us a fine bowl of soup, but, you know, if we just had a potato, den de soup would be outstanding.'

"Whereupon the lady said, 'Well, I do happen to have just one potato in my pantry.'

"After adding the potato to the pot the traveler proclaimed, 'Yes, ma'am, dis soup gon' be mighty good, but, you know, if we just had a piece of meat, den it would be delicious.'

"The lady jumped to her feet and said, 'Guess what, I do have one small piece of meat.'

"A little while later while dey both were sitting at the table enjoying de soup de lady said, 'This is some very good soup. And just think, we made it from nothing but water and a magic nail.'"

Jake stopped talking and I realized the story was over. I also figured there was some kind of hidden meaning in it and he was waiting for me to tell him what I thought it was.

My feelings were confirmed when he asked, "All right, Mister Ted, what do you think dat story means?"

"That people hide their food?"

Jake chuckled and said, "Dat too, but something more—think about it some."

I did, and then said, "The traveler tricked the lady into giving him some food?"

"Yes he did, but then he shared it with the lady. The main point is dat a smart man, a resourceful man, can always figure out a way to find hisself a bite to eat. So, don't you be worrying about old Jake, 'cause I'll be all right."

I wanted to spend more time with Jake, but I knew it was getting on toward midafternoon. Pretty soon my cousin Robert would be driving my mother and Fred home. If they found me on the road I'd have to explain where I had been, so I said good-bye to Jake, sneaked through the woods, and started walking toward home.

MY FATHER HADN'T SEEN ME coming down the road. He was on the front porch skinning squirrels and singing a mournful sounding song. I heard two lines of the tune before he saw me. It went like this:

"All around the water tank

"Just waiting for the train . . ."

When he saw me he stopped singing and asked, "Where's your mother and your brother?"

"They're visiting Uncle Curtis. I wanted to come on home and see if you got a turkey."

"Naw, I saw a big old gobbler, but I wasn't able to call him up. He outsmarted me today, but I'll get him sooner or later."

I had been turkey hunting with him before. He would scrape a piece of slate across a small wooden box he had made out of cedar, imitating the sound of a hen turkey, drawing the gobbler in close enough for the kill with his shotgun. All the while you had to sit hidden and motionless for a very long time, ignoring the bug bites and cramps. Then the sudden blast of the shotgun would make me just about jump out of my skin. Still, it was better than going to church. He always cut the beards off the big birds and gave them to me. I kept them in a cigar box underneath my bed.

"What's that song you were singing about?"

"Oh, it's about a man, a hobo, hanging around the water tank beside the railroad track because he knows the train will stop there. While it's stopped he's gonna sneak into a box car and travel on down the line to some place where he might find some kind of work."

Jake was right! White folks could sing the blues. My father had just been singing them and didn't even know it.

He kept dressing those squirrels while he talked. I looked into the pan of murky water and saw six skinned and gutted carcasses floating there. I knew that later my mother would cut them up with her butcher knife, roll them in flour, drop them into hot grease, and fry them up crispy and brown. Then she would make the gravy and drop the fried pieces of squirrel into it. While it bubbled away on the stove, she would bake the big biscuits. Eventually we would burst them open, cover them with gravy, and eat them with the fried squirrel. I liked the back legs. It wasn't turkey, but squirrel was good.

"Where's Ned?" I asked, while following my father from the front porch to the kitchen.

He set the pan containing our dinner on the table and answered, "He's gone back in the woods with a bucket. He found a honey tree and he's gone back to rob it."

My brother Ned was good at finding a honey tree, which was a hollow tree with a wild bee hive inside it. The bees gathered pollen from the wild flowers in the woods and the fields, resulting in the production of the most delectable honey to ever touch your mouth. I know how he captured the honey—I had been with him when he did it. He would build a small fire around the tree, throw some wet leaves on the fire, and the smoke would drive the bees away. While they were away he would scoop the honeycombs out with his hands, deposit them into a bucket and be gone before the bees returned. He never got stung and always brought home the honey.

Today was no exception. After a while I saw him emerging from the edge of the woods lugging a five-gallon bucket, which he set on the front porch. He was smoky and sticky, so I dipped water into the wash pan for him. While he was washing up he said to me, "Taste and see if it is good and sweet."

I dug my hand into the bucket, tore off a piece of honeycomb and stuffed into my mouth, and started chewing. My mouth was a flower garden. I chewed until there was nothing left but a hunk of wax, which I spat out in the yard.

"Well?" Ned asked.

"It's great," I said, licking my fingers.

Later my mother squeezed the honey from the combs and had six quarts of golden liquid on the table at supper time. Besides the squirrel gravy on the biscuits, we also had the nectar of the gods, thanks to my brother Ned, the bee hunter.

After supper, as we were all sitting around the table, my mother asked, "Well, how was everything?"

I said, "It was a lot better than nail soup," then I got up and left the table with everyone staring at me.

5

Snakes

Monday was a work day for everyone. My mother began doling out chores right after breakfast. We needed corn meal, so Ned's job was to shuck and shell twenty-five pounds of dried corn, which he would put in a cloth sack, drape the sack over his shoulder, and carry it to the mill to be ground into meal. No money was involved. The miller kept five pounds and Ned would return home with twenty pounds. I had been to the mill with him before. It was a long walk, several miles past Miss Lena's store on the way to Coffeeville. This wasn't such a tough job for Ned because he was fifteen years old, big, and strong; besides, he liked to visit and talk with the folks at the mill while waiting for the corn to be ground. At one time the mill had been on the creek near my hiding place under the wooden bridge. Then it was water-powered, but now it was run by a motor like the one at the sawmill, just not nearly as big.

Much to Fred's sorrow he was assigned to pull weeds in our garden. There were long rows of peas, green beans, butter beans, okra, squash, tomatoes, and corn.

When I heard my task I knew that we would be picking and shelling peas and butter beans for the next few days. My job was to wash the jars my mother would use to preserve the vegetables. Soon they would be on the shelves next to her stove, along with the wild blackberries and blueberries we had picked earlier in the year. These were used to make cobblers and pies during the winter months, but before summer was over there would also be jars of apples, peaches, pears, fig preserves, and all kinds of jellies and jams.

It was fun washing those glass jars. There were pints, quarts, and half-gallons. I was furnished with two foot-tubs of water, one hot and soapy, the other clean and clear. I used a small mop attached to a piece of wire to scrub the inside of the jars, plunged them into the clear water to rinse them, then turned them upside down on the table to drain.

I was finished long before my brothers. I decided to see if I could help Ned. Shucking and shelling corn was a better job than pulling weeds in the hot garden. He had finished removing the tough shucks from the ears of dried corn and was sitting on a bench just inside the open door of the corn crib, bending over the corn-shelling machine. This wonderful contraption was a wooden box with an iron cone attached to the inside. Inside the cone were metal teeth which ripped the dry kernels from the cob while you pushed the ear of corn down into the cone and turned the crank on the outside of the box. My father had traded a cypress skiff boat for it. He was a carpenter by trade, and a good one; except there was nothing to build around where we lived. But sometimes a cypress log would show up at the sawmill. When this happened he would keep the lumber from it to build his fishing boats, which he would always trade for something we needed.

I pushed the ears of corn down into the cone while Ned turned the crank until he decided he had enough. I held a sack open while he scooped the grains out of the box and deposited them into the sack. When I stepped out of the corn crib to the ground below something long and black slithered between my bare feet. Horrified, I yelled, "Snake!"

I grabbed a garden hoe that was leaning against the corn crib and began frantically chopping at the snake.

"Stop!" Ned yelled. "Don't kill it!"

But I kept chasing the snake until it circled back under the corn crib to safety. I could feel the tiny hairs on my arms standing up and see the chill bumps surrounding them. Ned took the hoe from my hand and said, "That was just a rat snake. You know we don't kill them because they keep the rats out of the corn."

"I don't care what kind it was. If I see it again, I'll kill it," I said. My voice and hands still shook.

"Well, you shouldn't, 'cause it won't hurt you," Ned said as he slung the sack of corn over his shoulder, on his way to the mill. Halfway up the road he turned and yelled, "Throw those shucks over the fence for the milk cow."

"I ain't going back in that crib," I yelled back.

"Then tell Fred to do it," he yelled again, turned and rounded the curve.

I got another scare from Fred who had sneaked up behind me and yelled, "Snake!"

I jumped, but realized what he was doing and said, "I ain't scared of no snake."

"Hey," he said, "tell you what—I'll feed the shucks to the

milk cow if you'll help me finish in the garden."

"Gonna take more than that."

"What else you want?"

"I want my marbles back."

"I'll give you half of them."

A few days ago he had won all twelve of my marbles, plus my "shooter." To play marbles we would draw a circle in the dirt, drop an equal amount of marbles into the circle, then we would kneel outside the circle and take turns shooting. To shoot you placed your shooter on the crook of your forefinger and flipped it with your thumb. Before the game, to see who shot first, we would lag our shooters at a line drawn in the dirt. The object of the game was to knock your opponent's marbles outside the circle. Any you knocked out then belonged to you, and you got to keep shooting as long as you kept knocking marbles out. Fred was real good at shooting marbles. He had a big rough bump on his right thumbnail from shooting so much.

"Plus my shooter," I demanded.

"All right, your shooter, too."

"Okay, but I ain't working around them okra plants."

Okra leaves made you sting and itch. I like to eat okra, but I didn't like weeding around the plants or cutting the pods off them.

Fred and I were both brown as berries from going half-naked all summer. Our blond hair had bleached almost white causing people to call us "cotton tops." So, today, while we toiled in the garden, the hot summer sun didn't even make us blink.

About noontime our mother came into the garden, inspected our work, approved it, and told us we could do as we pleased for a while. After washing up on the front porch we sat down to our dinner of butter beans, hot cornbread, and a glass of sweet milk. Before we got up from the table our mother reminded us that today was "egg day."

We gathered eggs daily from the chicken house which was inside a fence to keep the chickens in and the foxes out—though Old Bill, our black and tan coonhound, usually kept foxes and other varmints away.

On Mondays, we usually had a surplus of about three dozen eggs which we took to Miss Lena's store and sold them to her for ten cents a dozen. She would then sell them for fifteen cents a dozen.

"I'll go," I immediately volunteered. There were no protests from Fred, which made me happy, because I had a plan.

"Can I wait and take them later today? I'm too tired to go right now."

"That'll be fine. Just don't forget."

I FOLLOWED FRED out to the wood pile where he had been making a toy log truck. He had nailed together strips of scrap lumber from the sawmill to form the body. For the cab, he had nailed on an empty Prince Albert tobacco can after cutting a strip into it and lifting it up to make it look like a seat. Behind the cab, across the body, he had attached two bolsters with nails partially driven into the tip of each one. The nails would keep the toy logs from rolling off the truck. Today, he was going to attach the wheels.

I held a small round hickory tree trunk firmly across the

chopping block while he used our father's handsaw to cut four wheels. I held the truck sideways while he nailed the wheels to the axles and worked them back and forth until they turned. Finally, he set the truck on the ground, tied a string around the front axle, and we headed toward the woods with our log truck tumbling along behind us.

We cut ourselves a toy logging road into a stand of small pines where we began to cut the first load of logs for the truck. When we began loading them on the truck I said, "We need a toy mule to drag the logs up to the truck for us."

Fred looked at me incredulously and said, "A mule is a living and breathing thing. I never heard of such. How the heck you gonna make a toy mule?"

We whiled away the hours without a care until I heard our mother calling me.

"I guess it's time to take the eggs. What you gonna do?" I asked Fred.

"I'm gonna look for some straight sticks to make arrows with. Stop by the sawmill and find some thin strips of wood and I'll make us both a bow tomorrow."

Before going into the house, I went to the special place where I hid my money. Our house sat on tall round wood blocks at each of the four corners, high enough off the ground that I could almost walk under it. I quickly scooted underneath and found the half-pint fruit jar which I kept tucked away on the top edge of the block near the rain barrel. While I was extracting four nickels I heard a thumping sound. Looking up, I saw Old Bill lying sleepily in the dry dirt. His wagging tail sent up puffs of dust as it thumped against the ground. I knew Old Bill would keep my secret.

I saw him yawn and heard him whining as I crawled from beneath the house.

The eggs were in a basket on the kitchen table. I looked at the big clock, saw that it was about twenty minutes before five o'clock, and thought, good, I have just enough time to get past Miss Lena's store before the sawmill shuts down for the day.

My mother was on the front porch with a churn between her knees, slowly, methodically churning the clabbered milk. That meant fresh butter for breakfast and probably a cake tomorrow night. She looked up as I was going down the steps with the basket of eggs and said, "Don't you be hanging around Miss Lena's the rest of the day."

"I may stop by Pa Will's for a little bit." He was her daddy and my grandfather. I knew she wouldn't fuss about that.

"You just be sure and have yourself home before dark."

"Yes ma'am," I answered, comforting myself with the fact that I had said "may."

I kept my eyes peeled for that snake as I walked past the corn crib.

Actually, I was scared to death of snakes, and there were a lot of them around. I was constantly lectured, warned, and educated about them, especially the poisonous ones. The cottonmouth moccasin and the big rattlesnakes were the ones to be really concerned about. But there was another kind of snake, a coachwhip, which everyone said was non-poisonous but that struck fear into my heart. This snake was long and shiny brown with a golden yellow belly, and the unique thing about it was that it could run along the ground with two-thirds of its body rising straight up in the air. I had heard people say that if one of them caught you it would wrap around you and whip you.

Earlier this summer I had taken the short cut through the woods to Pa Will's house rather than the road. I was almost there when this giant coachwhip snake came tearing out of the tall weeds heading straight toward me. It seemed like it was raised up in the air so far it was taller than me, and I could see its red eyes and forked tongue. It felt like that snake chased me forever, but I outran it. By the time I got to my grandfather's house it was nowhere to be seen.

I HEARD THE HIGH-PITCHED whine of the big saw blade as it bit into a log after I passed the store and entered the woods with my eggs. Carefully, I counted out a dozen into a nest I formed with my hands in the pine straw. Then I covered them with more straw with hopes that no egg-sucking varmint would find them before I returned.

By the time I entered the store the sawmill had shut down and all the workers had departed. When Miss Lena counted out the eggs she asked, "What's wrong with your mother's chickens?"

"Ma'am?"

"There's only two dozen eggs here."

"I guess them hens were just lazy this week."

"Well, fine, then. Here's twenty cents for your momma. You take care and don't lose it."

"Yes, ma'am," I called out as I went through the door.

6

Bullies

I returned to the sawmill by my usual route, stopping to retrieve the dozen eggs on the way. I found Jake sitting on his usual block of wood, staring into his fire. But something seemed wrong. He didn't flash his big toothy smile when he saw me. He just said, "Hey, Mister Ted. What you got in dat basket? Mo' fried chicken, I hopes."

"No chicken, but I brought you a dozen fresh eggs," I said as I held the basket out for him to see the light brown globes.

He picked up one of the eggs, caressed it, and said, "Lawd a-mercy, dese sho be some beautiful eggs. I think I gonna scramble me up a mess of 'em tonight. No need to wait for morning."

Jake went into the tar paper shack and returned with an empty coffee can. He carefully removed the eggs from the basket, handling them like jewels as he placed them in the can. "I know yo' momma be looking for her basket back," he said. "I sho does 'preciate de eggs, Mister Ted."

He did seem appreciative, but Jake just wasn't his buoyant self. His smile faded too quickly and he seemed dejected despite the fresh eggs. We sat in silence for a few moments, then I couldn't stand it any longer. "Jake, you feeling bad?" I asked.

"Naw, I feels fine. It's just that I believes we got us a problem."

"What kind of a problem?"

"I had some more visitors late yesterday, after you left."

"Who?"

"Does you know a family of black folks who lives about three miles down de road towards Coffeeville?"

"No, I don't think so."

"Dey say dey chops and picks cotton for yo' Uncle Curvin."

"Oh, yeah, I know them. They got a boy who looks about my age."

"Dat's dem. De boy's name is Poudlum."

"Poudlum? What kind of a name is that?"

"It just a nickname. I don't know where it come from. His real name is Oleander. De family name is Robinson. Dey owns forty acres of land which been in de family since after the Civil War—when some lucky black folks got forty acres and a mule."

"Why did they come see you?"

"Dey heard I was here and dey just looking for advice and comfort."

"Then why do we have a problem?" I asked.

"I walked on home wid 'em last night, had supper wid 'em, and dey told me why yo' preacher was spouting all that hateful stuff in church Sunday."

"Jake, how could they know why Brother Benny was saying all that stuff?"

"Dey say he was put up to it by dis fella who owns everything around here—the fields, the timberland, Miz Miss Lena's store, and even dis here sawmill. I believe dey said his name wuz Creel, and—"

"Old Man Cliff Creel?" I interrupted.

"Yeah, dat's what dey called him."

"Why would he want the preacher to say all that?"

"'Cause he wants all de white folks to get stirred up and help him run dem off dey land."

"Why would he do that?"

"Because of de timber on it. Of the forty acres, only about ten acres farmland. De rest is virgin timber. I walked around and looked some. Dey is some huge hardwood and cedar trees, some of 'em over two hundred years old. I figures dat timber is worth a lot of money."

"So, Old Man Cliff Creel wants their land so he can cut down the trees for lumber?"

"Dat's what de Robinson family thinks, Mister Ted, and I tends to agree wid 'em. Dey say Mr. Creel has been trying to buy de land for several years."

"Why don't they just sell it to him?"

"Well, he ain't offering to buy no more. But dey got no other place to go, and dey wants to stay on the land. 'Pears he intends to drive 'em off."

"Tell them to just stay then."

"It ain't dat easy. Besides dat stuff the preacher be saying, dey's a heap of bad things been happening to 'em."

"Like what?"

"Dis spring, just before time to break up de ground for de crops, dey found dey mule dead one morning. Dey say he was a good mule, fairly young wid nothing wrong with him. Dey 'spects somebody might've poisoned him."

"Good Lord! Why would somebody want to poison a mule?"

"So dey couldn't get de crops in the ground."

"What'd they do?"

"Dey took what money dey had, borrowed a few more dollars from Mr. Creel, and bought another mule. Dey got de crops in all right, but ain't been able to pay him back, so last week he come and took dey milk cow away. All dem children, and dey ain't got no milk."

"I don't see how he could do that?"

"He trick 'em. Dey thought dey had until dey cotton crop come in to pay, but he had a paper dey signed that dey would give up the cow if the money hadn't been paid back by last week."

I thought about what a mean and selfish person Old Man Cliff Creel was and wished I could figure out someway to stop his unkind ways. The only thing I could think of at the moment was to take the Robinson family some milk, but I resolved to ponder on it more.

"Jake, what do you think is going to happen to 'em?"

"Dey might be all right. Dey gon' be picking cotton fo' yo' Uncle Curvin to pick up a little money, den, once dey get der own cotton crop to de gin, dey should be able to pay de taxes on dey land."

"They have to pay taxes on their land?"

"Oh, yes, sir—got to pay dem taxes."

"What happens if they don't?"

"Den de county will sell de land on the courthouse steps to de highest bidder, and I 'spects Mr. Creel would be waiting wid his big fat wallet."

JAKE HELPED ME go through the scrap lumber pile until we found two thin strips of hardwood suitable to make bows so Fred and I could shoot our arrows. Then I said good-bye to him while he was spooning lard into his skillet to scramble himself some eggs. I came through the woods, arrived at the store, laid my basket and wood strips down and went inside. I took a NuGrape soda from the drink box, and asked Miss Lena for one of the big coconut cookies from the jar sitting on the counter.

"That's a nickel for the drink and a penny for the cookie," she said.

When I handed her the money she asked, "You're not spending your momma's egg money, are you?"

"No, ma'am. See here, I got her money," I answered, holding out my hand to show her I still had twenty cents. Back outside, realizing I had too much to carry, I eliminated one item by eating the cookie. Then I looped my left arm through the handle of the egg basket, grabbed the wood strips, and with my drink in my right hand, started toward home.

When I rounded the corner from Center Point Road onto Friendship Road, I stopped and set everything down onto the hard-baked clay road while I drained the Nu-Grape. It wasn't as big as a Nehi, but it was my favorite—a carbonated grape drink. I decided to hide the empty bottle because it was worth a penny. I noticed a pile of leaves in the ditch so I just pitched the bottle into the middle of the pile. The moment the bottle hit the leaves that coachwhip came bursting out of the ditch, up on its tail, coming straight toward me. I remained frozen for a split second, every tiny hair on my body standing straight up. I broke out of my frozen state of fear when it reached the center of the road. I raced down that road on my bare feet with every ounce of energy I could muster. Somewhere along the way that snake must have given up, for when I reached Merle and Earl Hicks' house, I glanced over my shoulder and it was gone. My daddy was sitting with the Hicks on their front porch. Evidently he had stopped to talk with them after work. He could tell by looking at me that something had happened and came rushing out into the road and scooped me up into his arms. There were stories about rabid foxes being about at that particular time. He asked me if I was being chased by one.

"No, sir. It was a snake. A coachwhip," I gasped.

He promptly found a big stick and walked with me back to the pile of leaves and told me to toss a rock into it. I did and immediately got behind him.

As soon as my rock hit the leaf pile that snake came tearing out again. My daddy went at it with his stick and I was amazed to see the snake turn around and hide in the leaves. That didn't save it, though, because Daddy rousted it out and beat it to death with his stick. Then he lifted the long, limp body on his stick and tossed it into the middle of the road. That's when he told me the snake was like a lot of people I would meet in my life. He said that when a bully came at you to stand your ground and the bully would turn and run. However, he added, it was always a good idea to have a big stick.

We walked back to Miss Lena's store where Daddy bought me another soda and a big cookie.

I loved him for killing the snake, for teaching me the lesson about bullies, but most of all for buying me another NuGrape and cookie.

When we walked out of the store there was my brother Ned with his sack of cornmeal. Daddy relieved him of it and we all walked on down Friendship Road toward home.

That night for supper we had the buttermilk which my mother had churned that day, along with cornbread. The buttermilk had a sharp fresh taste and little hunks of butter floating in it. I had watched my mother mix the newly ground meal with buttermilk and two eggs before she put it into a black skillet and slid it into the wood stove. It came out of the oven brown and crunchy, a warm and welcome companion to the cool buttermilk.

I PREDICTED CORRECTLY that we would be picking and shelling green peas and butter beans soon. On Tuesday morning, right after breakfast, my mother herded Ned, Fred, and me into her garden. We filled basket after basket. When the picking was all done we moved to the front porch where the shelling began.

Even though we hated the work that went with it, my mother's garden was a wonderful place that produced much of our food. It was completely organic. She fertilized it with horse manure and inspected each plant every day, crushing any worm or bug that had dared invade.

Toward the end of each February, the onions, English peas, and potatoes would be planted. By the end of April we would be eating a big pot of those tender early peas cooked with red new potatoes with dumplings. Then the summer garden, which we were enjoying now, would be planted. Later in the year, she would put in the fall garden of turnips, mustard greens and collards, cabbage, and more onions.

But today, after shelling peas and beans for hours, nobody was happy about anything in the garden, especially Fred. He had been fidgeting and complaining for an hour. "My hands are raw. I can't shell anymore," he said.

"All right," Momma said. "You and Ted go play. Me and Ned will finish shelling the rest. Y'all take all these hulls and feed them to the cow before you wander off."

While we were throwing the hulls over the fence I was puzzled to see Fred stuff a handful into his pocket. Then he said, "Come on, grab the log truck, and let's go.

"But what about making the bows? I brought some hardwood strips from—"

"Forget the bows, we're going to haul some logs."

"But why?"

I could not believe what came out of his mouth when he answered, saying, "I caught us a toy mule."

"What? But you said there was no such thing."

"I changed my mind, now come on."

In lower Alabama there is a type of turtle which lives on dry land, never going near water, and it eats plants instead of fish. It also burrows a slanted hole into the ground as its den; therefore, it's called a "gopher" turtle.

When we arrived at our playground in the woods, there

was a gopher tied to a tree. Fred had drilled a hole into the rear overhang of its shell and run a piece of cord through it. The turtle started hissing and sucked its head into its shell when we knelt on the ground in front of it.

Fred put the pea hulls on the ground in front of the turtle and said, "Now, let's move away from it a bit."

After a few minutes its head slowly snaked out of its shell and began munching on the pea hulls. After it had eaten Fred took the cord loose from the tree and attached it to one of the play logs we had cut. Then he took a stick and began tapping on the gopher's shell, and to my amazement it began dragging the little log up the hill toward our toy log truck. I could hardly believe it, we had probably the only toy mule in the whole wide world.

We spent the entire afternoon imitating the grown loggers we knew and admired, playfully performing the only occupation we knew to aspire to.

It was almost dark when we released our toy mule and followed it as it shuffled back to its den. As it disappeared into the ground I asked Fred, "What if we want to use him again?"

"Don't worry," he replied. "I'll just put some pea hulls in front of his hole and when he gets hungry I'll catch him again."

THE NEXT THREE days passed uneventfully, then on Friday night not long after I had fallen asleep, I was awakened by angry voices. Ned and Fred remained sound asleep but I slid out of bed and put on my jeans. I couldn't make out what the voices were saying, but their tone was definitely angry.

I quietly opened the wooden shutter which served as a window, lifted myself through and silently dropped to the ground in the rear of the house next to the rain barrel.

I scooted underneath the house and started crawling toward the front side. Despite the bright moonlight, it was pitch black under the house, causing me to crawl blindly. About halfway, my hands landed on something soft and warm. I jerked back and bumped my head on the floor above. My fear disappeared when I heard Old Bill whine and thump his tail on the ground. "Quiet, boy," I whispered as I patted him and crawled around him and continued toward the front side of the house.

The voices were becoming clearer now. I heard my father say, "Are you real sure about that, S. T.?"

He was talking to S. T. Brooks who worked with him at the sawmill. I saw his old truck parked in the yard as I slid down onto my belly and peeked out. I recognized two other men, Elvin Hodge and Garrett Findley, who were also sawmill workers. The four of them were gathered around the hood of the truck.

Things got quiet for a moment and when I strained my eyes I saw why. They were drinking whiskey. Silently they passed the bottle from one to the other.

When the bottle had made its round I heard Mr. Brooks say, "I tell you, J. D., it's a fact. They gonna close the mill down in about three weeks and ain't none of us gonna have a job."

Elvin Hodge said, "I think he's right. They ain't been one load of logs delivered to the mill this week. There's about a three-week supply on the yard. Once they're gone, I think we're gone."

The secret was out! They knew the mill was closing. I watched silently while the bottle made another round.

Garrett Findley was the last one to take a long pull from the bottle. When he lowered it from his mouth he said, "The mill is definitely gonna close. What really galls me is that nigger Jake is gonna still have a job for six weeks after it closes. That job could have gone to one of us."

"How do you know that?" Mr. Brooks quickly asked.

"I overheard Blossom discussing it with Jake. Telling him it would take about that long to get the lumber hauled away, the mill broken down and the parts hauled away."

"That just ain't right. Gimme that bottle," Mr. Brooks said. "What do the rest of y'all think?"

My father didn't speak, just took the bottle, drank and passed it on to Elvin Hodge, who took a long drink and said, "I bet if we go over to the mill and roust that nigger out of his shack, run him on out of here, then one of us would have that job."

"That's a damn good idea," Mr. Brooks said. "Y'all load up and let's take a ride over to the sawmill."

I was horrified as I watched the four of them pile into the truck. I heard the engine roar to life and saw the lights come on and the truck start moving away.

I had to go warn Jake!

7

Milk and Butter

Warning Jake was wishful thinking, but I tried. I pushed Old Bill aside and hit the trail through the woods on the run, feeling the tree limbs on each side brushing me as I raced along. I came out at the top of the little hill and knew I was too late as I saw the taillights of the truck disappear over the crest of the big hill.

Suddenly I realized there was nothing I could do except go back home, and the moon wasn't shining so bright on the trail through the woods. I chose the road, but ran hard all the way. Back at the window to our room, I had to sit still until my breathing was normal. Then I crawled back through the window, heard my brothers' steady breathing, quietly slid into bed, and eventually dropped off into a troubled sleep. Everything seemed normal the next morning. I had heard my father when he left for work and nobody seemed disturbed around the breakfast table.

I left home early. Besides my paper route, I had a lot to do that day. I arrived at the row of mail boxes on Center Point

Road before the mail rider, and while waiting for his arrival I shaded my face from the morning sun with my hand and looked hard toward the sawmill. Everything sounded and looked normal. The big saw blade screamed in protest as a log was fed into it. I could see men moving logs around and stacking lumber. Then I spotted Jake. He was sliding a stack of slabs down the ramp toward the fire. I watched them fall off the end of the ramp, float through the air, then hit the fire spewing sparks and flaming chunks of wood into the air. When I looked back up Jake had disappeared, gone for another load. I couldn't imagine what had happened last night, but he seemed okay.

I was going to reverse my route today, go east first and then west because I knew the Robinsons lived west toward Coffeeville. I spotted a dust cloud up the road and knew my papers would be here shortly.

Mrs. Blossom went through the same ritual as last week, except I didn't get a fried chicken leg. While I was packaging up the pay envelopes she said, "There was some kind of commotion down at the mill last night."

"What happened?"

"Not sure. A truck drove in there during the middle of the night and we heard a lot of loud talking."

"Did Mr. Blossom go down there?"

"Lord, no, child. That man's scared of his own shadow. Whoever it was went away after a little while. Mr. Blossom came back up to the house after the mill started up this morning and said everything was fine. I'll just be so proud when— Well, I know you got your papers to sell, so you run along now, and don't lose your money."

"No, ma'am, I won't. Thank you, ma'am," I said on my way out with thirteen nickels in my pocket. I could hardly wait to talk to Jake, but that would have to wait until later in the day.

I made my rounds without stopping to talk much, and was back at Miss Lena's store by eleven o'clock, an hour ahead of schedule. I was getting hungry, but I didn't stop, thinking that I was a resourceful person and could find some nail soup somewhere on down the road.

I knew I had reached that place when I saw Uncle Bud's house in the distance. He and my great-aunts, Minnie and Sadie, were in their rocking chairs on the front porch, rocking away. They hadn't seen me yet. I stopped and observed for a while.

As usual, they were dipping snuff. Every few rocks they would stop at the end of the forward motion, lean forward, and spit great dark brown streams over the edge of the porch. I counted the rocks between spits and it was eight to twelve. They were always rocking on the porch, always dipping snuff. The field behind their house had long ago been taken over by weeds and saplings, since they were too old to work it anymore. They did maintain a small garden. I realized that I didn't even know which one of my aunts was married to Uncle Bud, but I supposed at their age it didn't really matter.

I knew I would have to endure the hugs and cheek pinching, but I also knew they would buy a paper, and I was hungry. Plus, I always did some small chore for them.

Today, they wanted me to draw a bucket of water from the well in the back yard.

When I came back into the kitchen, lugging the pail of water, there was a plate on the table for me. The plate contained a biscuit with a big slice of cured ham in it. I knew it would make me thirsty later in the day, but I liked their ham. There was also a helping of bread pudding. I washed it all down with cool fresh water from a glass which they had originally bought full of peach snuff.

"You want another biscuit, sugar boy?" Aunt Minnie asked. "No, ma'am, I'm full. Thank you." That's what all my aunts called me—"sugar boy." I never knew why.

"We was about to give up on you," Aunt Sadie said.

"Yes, ma'am, I'm late because I reversed my route today."

"Why did you do that?" Uncle Bud asked.

"Uh, just to make things different," I lied.

As I was leaving they split up the *Grit* paper into three parts, sat back down in their chairs on the porch, loaded up their bottom lips with fresh dips of snuff, and resumed rocking.

I PASSED OLD Man Cliff Creel's house on my right, stayed on the opposite of the road, and walked fast. Less than a half mile on down the road on my left was the wagon path which had to lead to the Robinsons' house, according to what Jake had said. I stopped to look down the path, but couldn't see anything except that it curved around a huge black walnut tree and disappeared. I knew I would be seeing what was around that curve in a while.

Another twenty minutes on down the road I reached my last stop, a small white farm house sitting in plain sight just a few steps off the road. There was a big pasture in the back with a small barn just inside the gate to the pasture. Mrs. Annie Pearl Wiggins lived there. She was a widow who made her living selling milk and butter produced by her five Jersey cows. I found her on the back porch churning milk. "Afternoon, Mrs. Annie Pearl."

She looked up from her churn and replied, "Howdy, boy. You running late today."

"Yes, ma'am, I got a late start." I felt bad about telling so many lies lately, but I knew I wasn't doing it to hurt anybody.

"It's just as well. I haven't had time to do no reading today. How's your mamma and them?"

"Everybody's fine, thank you, ma'am," I said as I laid her paper on the edge of the porch. She reached into her apron pocket and flipped me a nickel. "Mrs. Annie Pearl, I need to buy a gallon of milk."

"Your momma's cow gone dry?"

"Uh, no ma'am. It's for somebody else."

"You want buttermilk or sweet milk?"

I thought for a few moments. Buttermilk was ten cents a gallon and sweet milk was fifteen cents a gallon, but I knew the Robinsons could drink half a gallon of sweet milk and then churn the other half and have themselves some buttermilk and some butter. "I'll take sweet milk," I answered while I stacked three nickels on the edge of the porch.

"It's in the springhouse. Go over there and get yourself a gallon."

The springhouse was a small structure built around a spring to keep the contents secure and cool in the water. The water was from a spring which bubbled up out of the ground and stayed cold all summer long. The spring had been boxed in with big wide boards on the sides. The bottom was white boiling sand which gave the appearance it was hot, but it was cold. We had a small spring like it, except we didn't have a house built around ours. There was a dipper hanging on the wall. I used it to have a long cool drink, then I lifted a gallon jar out of the water and walked back into the backyard. "Good-bye, Mrs. Annie Pearl," I said.

"Who you taking that milk to, son?"

I had hoped she wouldn't ask me that question.

When she saw my hesitation she said, "I need to know where my jar is. I'll be wanting it back."

I knew I had to tell and I couldn't see that it would do any harm. "You know the Robinsons, the colored family that lives up the road a piece?"

"I've seen them come and go. Why in the world are you taking milk to them?"

"'Cause they don't have any."

"Oh, so their cow is the one that's dry."

"No, ma'am, Old Man Cliff Creel took their milk cow."

"What for?"

"They owed him some money, couldn't pay him, and he had made them sign a paper."

"Why that lowdown polecat. One of these days he's going to get what's coming to him. You wait right there."

She walked over to the springhouse and went inside. She returned with a pound of butter wrapped up tight in wax paper, stuck it inside my *Grit* paper bag, and said, "You take this to them—no charge. Tell them they can get all the milk they need from me, won't have to pay me until they sell their cotton crop, and don't have to sign no paper, either."

"I'll do that, Mrs. Annie Pearl. Thank you, ma'am, and I'm sure they will thank you, too."

"You best be getting on up the road before that butter melts."

The gallon of milk got heavy after a while. I kept switching it from arm to arm. I turned off Center Point Road and passed the big black walnut tree, rounded the curve of the road, and found myself in the middle of a huge cotton field. The road continued through the field and once again disappeared over the top of a hill. When I reached the top of the hill I saw the house. It looked a lot like mine, constructed of unpainted pine boards, except it was larger and cotton plants grew right up to within a few feet of it. There was a dull amber reflection from the sun off the rusty tin roof, nestled in a sea of white. I saw no sign of anybody or any type of motion as I walked down the hill toward the house. I was getting real close when a big black dog suddenly came charging at me, snarling and growling. I was almost as much afraid of mean dogs as I was of snakes. There was no place to run. I knew he could catch me before I could get back up the road to the woods. If I ran into the cotton patch the stalks would slow me down more than the dog. He was close enough now so that I could see his hackles standing up, then to my great relief he was abruptly jerked sideways by the chain attached to his collar. I hadn't seen the chain.

As my fear receded I gave thanks for the chain and for the fact that I had stopped in the woods a few minutes ago, for if I hadn't, then surely I would have peed on myself.

"Where you going wid yo' milk?"

The voice came from just inside the front screen door. I couldn't see who it was, but the voice sounded as if it would match the boy who I figured was about my age. "Is that you, Poudlum?" I asked.

"How you knows my name?"

"Jake told me."

"Jake from de sawmill?"

"Yeah. He came to see y'all a few days back."

Poudlum came out onto the front porch and said, "I knows yo' name, too. You is Mister Ted. Come on up on de porch."

The dog was sitting, but still growling. "Uh, you want to call off your dog?"

Poudlum scampered down the steps, ripped a limb off a cotton plant, rapped it across the dog's head, and said, "Shut up, Buster."

The dog whined, put its tail between its legs and ran underneath the porch.

"Buster won't hurt you."

"Wouldn't have thought that a minute ago," I said as I walked up on the porch and set the jar of milk on the edge, still keeping a sharp eye out for Buster.

"This milk is for you and your family. Jake told me how y'all had lost your cow."

"How come you bring us milk?"

"'Cause I knew you didn't have none."

"Jake said you a fine fella. I s'pose he right. You got two older brothers, too, don't you?"

"Yeah, you got any?"

"I got six brothers and sisters. Dey all older dan me."

"Where's everybody?"

"Dey all picking cotton over on de back side of the field. I was, too. Just come up to de house to get 'em a bucket of water, den I heard Buster raising cain."

"Y'all gonna be picking cotton for my Uncle Curvin?"

"Un huh, 'spect we be starting next week."

"How do you pick all this cotton and his too?"

"I don't know—we just does."

"Poudlum!" a female voice yelled from behind the house.

"Uh-uh," Poudlum said while I watched as his eyes grew wide. "Dat's my momma."

A tall, imposing black woman rounded the corner of the house saying, "Boy, where dat water—" She stopped in her tracks when she saw me, then said, "Who does we have here?"

"Dis is Mister Ted, Momma. You know, Jake's friend."

I saw her eyes dart to the milk sitting on the porch. "We ain't got no money fo' no milk," she said.

"Mister Ted brought us dat milk, Momma. Don't need no money."

She turned back toward me and asked, "Why you do dat?"

I couldn't understand why they kept asking why. It was pretty simple to me. "Jake told me about Old Man Cliff Creel taking y'all's milk cow. Oh, I almost forgot, Mrs. Annie Pearl sent y'all a pound of butter, too." I reached into my *Grit* bag for the butter and laid it on the porch next to the milk. It was beginning to get soft.

Then I went on to tell the offer Mrs. Annie Pearl had extended about selling them milk on credit.

"She say dat fo' shore?"

"She sure did. Well, I got to be getting on up the road," I said.

Poudlum began jumping up and down and said, "Momma, can I please walk wid him, just up to de main road."

"Sho you can, but first put dat milk and butter in de spring. I'll take the water back to the field. 'Spect dey be mighty thirsty by now."

Mrs. Robinson turned toward me again and said, "Mister Ted, you come again, anytime. When cold weather get here and we be making syrup, we gon' save a bucket just fo' you. And may de good Lawd take a liking to you. And you, Poudlum, I see you back in de cotton field."

With that she turned and was gone. Once we had secured the milk and butter, Poudlum and I were ready to start walking up toward the road when Buster got brave again. He came out from underneath the porch with a rumbling growl heading straight toward me. This time, I tore a limb off the cotton stalk and charged him. He turned and ran back underneath the porch. Buster was a bully and a coward, just like the coachwhip. My father had been right. I resolved to get myself a real good stick and keep it with me all the time.

"You come play with me sometime?" Poudlum asked.

"When?'

"Sunday afternoon. We be picking cotton de rest of de time for a while."

"I don't know," I answered.

"If you will, den I'll show you a secret I found in de woods."

I was only half listening to him, walking fast because I was anxious to get to the sawmill and talk to Jake about last night. "What kind of secret?" I asked.

I stopped dead in my tracks, and could not believe my ears, when I heard what came out of Poudlum's mouth.

8

The Bootlegger

In Alabama in 1948 the only place you could legally buy whiskey was at a special store operated by the Alabama Alcoholic Beverage Control Board. Not all counties had ABC stores because counties could vote whether to be "wet" or "dry." We lived in a "dry" county, so anyone living around Coffeeville would have to travel many miles to buy legal alcohol.

Every time an election to go "wet" came around the bootleggers and the preachers would join forces and go to work campaigning against the issue. The bootleggers did it for the obvious reason—to maintain their flow of tax-free profits. The preachers wanted to save people from temptation and they would revive their sermons on the evils of alcohol, all the while taking huge donations from the bootleggers, and an occasional bottle of whiskey.

In most rural counties, the "drys" always won, and even though it was illegal, a person could buy a bottle of whiskey with greater ease than in a county where it was legal. There were only two things a bootlegger had to be concerned about: an honest sheriff being elected, and the protection of his identity. On the totem pole of society, a known bootlegger was barely above dirt; therefore, it was always a deep dark secret of who he really was.

This is why I was so astounded when I heard Poudlum say, "I found de place where Old Man Cliff Creel makes his whiskey."

"You what?!"

"I knows where his still is."

"Are you telling me Old Man Cliff Creel is a bootlegger?"

"Uh huh."

"How long you been knowing this?"

"Tomorrow will be two weeks."

"You told your momma and daddy?"

"Naw, I ain't told nobody—I be too scared."

I still could hardly believe what I had heard, but if it was true, it was good news indeed. I knew that old man was evil, and now I might be able to prove it. "Poudlum, that's a great secret. Don't tell nobody. Did you see that old man at the still?"

"Sho did. Saw him box up bottles of whiskey and tote 'em away through the woods."

"Tomorrow then. You'll show me where it is tomorrow?"

"See our cotton house way over yonder, close to de edge of the woods?" He pointed.

"Yeah."

"We'll meet behind it a little while after dinner."

"All right, around two o'clock. I'll see you there. Now, I got to go."

"Bye, Mister Ted."

"Just Ted, okay? Bye, Poudlum. I'll see you tomorrow."

BACK OUT ON Center Point Road, I was thirsty and thinking about getting to Miss Lena's and wrapping my hand around a cold longneck Nehi. But first, I had to walk back by that intimidating house. Old Man Creel's new Chevrolet was in his car shed. Another car that hadn't been there when I passed by earlier was in the driveway. Squinting my eyes against the glare of the sun, I made it out to be Brother Benny's car. What could the preacher be doing there, I wondered. I could hear voices coming from the back yard but couldn't make out the words. And I sure was curious to know what they were taking about.

There was a wire fence grown over with vines and bushes towards the back of the house. I figured if I could crawl up next to it, then I might be able to hear what Old Man Creel and Brother Benny were saying.

I walked on far enough to get out of sight, crossed the road and entered the woods. I stashed my *Grit* bag at the base of a big loblolly pine tree then started back toward the house. I dropped to my belly at the edge of the woods and crawled through a strip of tall brown grass until I got to the fence. Then I began working my way toward the back of the house under the cover of the grass and vines. The voices grew louder and clearer and I knew I was close enough when I heard Old Man Cliff Creel say, "That was a mighty fine sermon you preached last Sunday, Brother Benny."

I slowly parted some of the thick vines until I had a small peephole. They were sitting at a table in the back yard under the shade of a chinaberry tree covered with clusters of purple flowers. It didn't seem right to me that those two men should get to sit under such a beautiful tree. I liked to watch chinaberry wood burn in the fireplace, where it kicked up red and green sparks. Brother Benny snapped me back to reality when he responded, "Why thank you, Mr. Creel. I plan to expound on it tomorrow by preaching about the listless drunken habits of the whole lot of them."

I licked my dry lips when I saw them raise their glasses and heard the clinking of ice. I figured they were drinking sweet tea until I saw Old Man Creel take a brown pint bottle and pour a portion into both glasses. Whiskey! There sat the preacher drinking whiskey and plotting against the Robinsons. Jake had been right.

"Good, that's real good, Brother Benny, but don't forget their nasty habits of stealing and not paying their debts. That bunch down the road tried to weasel out of paying money they owed me, but I didn't let 'em get away with, no sir. I went and took their cow which they had signed over as collateral. Hell, I'm a businessman, not some fraternal nigger-loving organization."

"Serves 'em right—the slackers," Brother Benny replied. "I suppose I should be going, need to work on my sermon," he said, draining his glass and rising to his feet. "I'll look forward to seeing you in the house of the Lord tomorrow."

"I'll be there, on the front row. Before you go, here's a donation. Wouldn't look right if I put this in the collection plate."

Old Man Creel also stood, dug deep into his pocket, came out with a big roll of money, and handed it to the preacher. Then he reached under the table, pulled a fresh bottle from a cardboard box and said, "Take this along with you too—just for medicinal purposes, of course."

That's when my luck ran out. It hadn't been my day for dogs. I saw a big mean-looking red bulldog come around the corner of the house. He had a huge head and strong square jaws, with a big stocky body. His nose was up in the air, sniffing. I knew right away that this dog was no bully and no coward. He was looking straight at the spot where I lay hidden, then he started trotting toward me with a menacing growl deep in his throat. I started crawfishing backwards as fast as I could without giving myself away. I wanted desperately to stand and run, but I knew I would be seen.

That dog hit the fence snarling and snapping. I knew I was in bad trouble if he got through.

As I was turning myself around on my belly so I could crawl forward, I heard Brother Benny say, "Looks like your dog has scared hisself up a rabbit, Mr. Creel."

"That ain't no rabbit. He wouldn't be acting like that. I'm going to get my shotgun and see what the hell's on the other side of that fence."

When I heard him say that, and heard that dog ripping at the wire with his big jaws, I figured I was a goner. But I just kept crawling and crawling until I was finally back into the woods where I could stand up and run. Snatching up my bag, I exited the woods and hit the road running as hard as I could, my feet kicking up puffs of dust behind me. I didn't stop until I got to Miss Lena's store.

I sat on the front steps for a while, catching my breath

and counting my blessings, before going inside to purchase a much-needed Nehi.

I HID THE empty bottle in the woods on the way to the sawmill. Empty soda bottles were money in the bank to me. I had about fifteen hidden near the store, each one worth a penny. I knew they were there if I needed money. Anxious for my rendezvous with Jake, not only to find out what happened last night, but also to tell him about the conversation I had just overheard, I hurried out of the woods straight toward his shack. There he was, sitting on his bench, whittling on a piece of wood. Looking up, he saw me, smiled real big and waved me over toward his bench.

I noticed he was brewing coffee in a big empty can. "What happened to your coffee pot?" I asked.

"It got busted up last night. Gots to get me a new one.."

"They didn't harm you last night, did they?"

"Naw. Only thing got harmed was my coffee pot. How you know about anything happening last night?"

After I told him my story he said, "I appreciate you trying to look out for me, but don't you worry cause old Jake been in some tight spots before, and I done learned how to look out for myself."

"What did they do?"

"Oh, they just come driving down here all liquored-up yelling for me. When dey couldn't find me dey busted my coffee pot, yelled a few threats, den dey just went on off home."

"How come they couldn't find you?"

"'Cause I have learned to anticipate what folks might do and to be prepared if dey do what I anticipate."

When he saw me looking at him questioningly, he went on, "I done loosened some boards on de back of de shack in case I don't want to come out of de front. So when I heard 'em coming I just slid out my back door and hid in yo' favorite place until dey left."

"Where?"

"Why, dey sawdust pile. I just burrowed myself down in it until nothin was showing 'cept my eyeballs."

We both laughed for a while, then I told him, "I'm proud nothing bad happened to you, especially since my daddy was one of them."

"You can still be proud of yo' daddy, 'cause he done come by and apologized to me dis morning. He say dey been drinking, done figured out de sawmill gon' close by de decrease in de flow of logs coming in, and some of dem done overheard Mr. Blossom talking 'bout it. Some of dem be upset 'cause I gon' have a job after it closes and dey ain't. Once I told 'em Mr. Blossom only pay me five dollars a week, dey say none of 'em want de job nohow."

I was glad to hear that about my father, but I didn't understand why Jake was getting paid so little, so I asked, "How come you only get paid five dollars a week? That ain't even half what the other men get paid. You do the same work they do."

"You tells me the answer to dat question."

"I don't know, that's why I asked you."

"I thinks you really don't know de answer, Mister Ted. I thinks dat 'cause you is innocent, so I gonna tell you. It be 'cause dey knows I has to take whatever job comes my way, no matter what de pay. So since some folks know dat I have no choice, den dey takes advantage of me."

"How come they can get away with that?"

"'Cause of folks like dat preacher and Mr. Creel making folks believe dat all black folks is lazy, shiftless, and dishonest. Dey wants to make folks believe dat just 'cause of de color of a person's skin, dat dey all be de same."

"That ain't right."

"Lawd, I wish you wuz a grown man. I believes you is enlightened."

"I need me a good stick, Jake."

"What you talking about?"

I told him the story about the coachwhip and the lesson my father had taught me about bullies and cowards.

"Dat's a good lesson, but sometimes you might need more dan a good stick."

I tended to agree with him after the near encounter with Old Man Creel's dog, but that would come later. I had so much to tell him, so I started at the beginning and told him about the milk and butter I had taken to the Robinsons' where I had been accosted by Buster.

"You is a charitable child, and yes, a good stick would've come in handy. I knows old Buster, and you is right about him."

I had thought about it for a while and decided to keep mine and Poudlum's secret, at least for the time being. At first I was suspicious that he had made the story up just to get me to come play with him, but that was before I had overheard the backyard conversation. Now I believed

Poudlum; but I wanted to see the moonshine still before I even thought about talking to Jake about it.

"That's not all, Jake. Listen to this." I proceeded to tell him about sneaking up behind Old Man Creel's house and the conversation I had overheard between him and Brother Benny. "So you see, Jake, you were right about why the preacher said what he did in church and who put him up to it."

"Yeah, and it sound like he gonna be spouting out more poison come tomorrow."

"Wait, there's more," I said, then I told him about that big mean red dog.

"Lawd, have mercy," he said. "De angels wuz looking after you today. I seen dat dog through de fence. Ifen he got a-holt of you, he would've torn you to pieces. Now, dat's an example of when you would need something more dan a good stick."

"Like what? I ain't got no gun. Couldn't walk around with it even if I did."

"Yo' momma got any dried hot peppers?"

I thought about the big bunch of dried hot red peppers hanging by a string on the wall behind her stove. I remembered seeing her snatch one from the bunch and crumble it into a pot of soup or chili. "Yeah, she's got a lot of them."

"Get yo' self one of dem little empty tin snuff cans. Plenty of 'em laying around on de ground up by de store. Take some of dem hot peppers and mash 'em up real fine. After mashing 'em up, don't touch yo' eyes or yo' privates until you wash yo' hands real good wid soap and water. Fill dat snuff can up wid de hot pepper and put it in yo' newspaper bag. Den, if any dog dat you can't handle wid a stick come after you, you use de pepper on 'em."

"How would I do that?"

"Say dat big dog had a gotten through de fence, den just fo' he gets to you, you toss de pepper in his mouth and face."

"That would stop him?"

"Sho would. He would start choking, snorting, whining, and scratching at his eyes."

"How you know all that?"

"Trust me, child. I been chased by some real bad dogs. In the meantime, let's find you a good temporary stick."

We rummaged around in the scrap pile until Jake found a stout piece of hickory about as long as I was tall. "Dis'll do until I can make you a proper stick."

I knew it was time to go. I had three papers left. "Do you want a paper, Jake," I asked.

"Sho do. Gotta see what's going on in de world," He said as he fished a nickel out and flipped it toward me. I caught it and said, "You don't have to pay. I've made plenty of money today."

"Oh, no. You has shared wid me and I gonna share wid you. I think one reason we understands each other so good is that you is just about as po' as I is."

As I entered the woods I could hear the music of Jake's guitar and him start singing, "Got dem old sawmill blues . . ."

9

The Still

On the way home, just past the Earl and Merle Hicks place, I turned down toward my Grandfather Murphy's house. He was my mother's daddy and the oldest person I knew. Everybody said he was close to ninety years old, but even he didn't know his exact age. His name was William Murphy, but everybody called him Pa Will. He had a dark complexion and brown eyes, like my mother and Ned. Momma said his hair used to be black as coal, just like hers. Now it was white as mine. My mother also said he was one-fourth Creek Indian, but he wouldn't own up to it. Like most other old folks, he spent a lot of time rocking and dipping snuff, which is what he was doing when I walked up to the edge of the porch and said, "Hey, Pa Will. How you feeling?"

"I'm tolerable, sonny boy."

"I brought you a *Grit* paper," I said, handing a copy up to him.

He took the paper and started fumbling around in his pockets looking for his eyeglasses. Once he found them he put them on, looked down at me and asked, "What you doing with that stick?"

"Just taking it along with me in case I run up on a snake or a mean dog."

"Smart boy," he said, seemingly to himself, while he unfolded the newspaper on his lap.

About that time my step-grandmother, Ernestine, known as Ma Tine, came out onto the porch.

"Hey, sugar boy," she said.

"Hey, Ma Tine."

She was a lot younger than my grandfather and for some reason my mother didn't like her, but she had always been real good to me.

"You want something to eat, hon?"

"No, ma'am, I just stopped by to bring Pa Will a paper. I got to be getting on home."

"Well, say hey to your momma and them."

"Yes, ma'am, I will," I said. Having paid my respects, I backed away from the porch and waved good-bye. I walked back up to Friendship Road and turned toward home.

I had only taken a few steps when I heard Fred yelling from behind me. "Hey, wait up," he called.

As he jogged toward me I could see the bag of marbles tied to his belt, swaying and jumping. I figured that not a kid within five miles had a marble left after today. In his hands, cupped against his chest, he carried several maypops.

"Where'd you get them maypops," I asked.

"Found 'em growing 'side the road a ways back. You want one?"

"Heck yeah," I answered, helping myself to two while his hands were tied up.

"Hey! I said one."

Maypops grew on a vine with white and purple flowers producing a wrinkled round fruit about the size of a peach. They turned yellow when they were ripe and had a tangy sweet meat inside the hulls. No one planted them. They just grew in the fields and beside the roads.

As we walked and munched Fred asked, "You sell all your papers?"

"All but two. Took one to Pa Will and I saved one for Momma. You win a lot of marbles?'

"About thirty."

"You ought to quit shooting marbles."

"How come?"

"'Cause ain't no money in it."

"Yeah there is."

"How? All you do is win marbles."

"Yeah, but then I sell 'em back," he said, reaching into his pocket to jingle his money.

"And then next Saturday you go win them back again?"

"You got it. Hey, Uncle Curvin came to the house after you left this morning. We start picking cotton on Monday morning."

"He say I could pick?"

"Yeah. We start on one side of the field. He said he had them Robinson niggers lined up to start on the other side."

Then tomorrow had to be the day to find out where the still was, I thought. Otherwise I would have to wait another week because everyone, including Poudlum, would be tied up picking cotton until then.

FRED COULDN'T DEVISE a way to get out of going to church the next morning, but he did the next best thing by coming up with a way for us to pass the time. Just before we went in he handed me a stubby pencil, then he quickly flashed a stack of tic-tac-toe diagrams he had drawn and then cut up into individual squares. "Let's go get a seat on the end of a pew, and save a little room between us. I'll slip a paper on the pew between us and we'll just play slow and easy so no one catches us."

We played the game for the whole hour. Before I knew it that whiskey-drinking preacher was starting the dismissal prayer. The entire service had been a blur to me.

I did remember that he had gotten the poisonous comments directed at the Robinsons into the sermon, but I was over that preacher. From now on, I would place no credence to anything he had to say, and maybe even expose him for what he was, along with Old Man Creel.

Now I was dreading going out the front door where he would be standing around talking to everyone. Fred saved me again. He tugged at my shirt sleeve and whispered, "Just hold back and let everybody get in front of us."

Once that happened, he slipped through the open window and disappeared. I did the same and dropped to the ground below. From there we circled around the crowd and waited for everyone on the back of Uncle Curtis's truck.

After cousin Robert drove us home, we had dinner and were free for the rest of the day. I was attempting to think up some kind of story about where I was going for the afternoon when Fred announced he was going to meet Quincy Woodard at Miss Lena's store; then they were going swimming at the cypress hole in the Satilfa Creek, and I was invited to come along. To get to the swimming hole you had to walk east on Center Point Road, cross the Mill Creek, then continue on for another half mile. It was a long walk. That was the excuse I used after we got to the store. I told Fred and Quincy, "I ain't going—it's too far to walk."

"Then what're you gonna do?" Fred asked.

"I'll probably just go visit Pa Will for a while, then go on back home." Here I was, lying again, I thought.

Fred studied me for a moment. I could tell he knew I was up to something, but he didn't push. "All right then, I'll see you back at the house." Once they were out of sight I started west, staying off the road, traveling through the edge of the woods all the way to the road leading to the Robinsons' house. Even then, I stuck to the woods, circling the cotton field until I came out at the back of the cotton house.

A cotton house is a small structure, usually ten feet by ten feet, made out of clap boards with a tin roof, used to store picked cotton until time to take it to the gin. Poudlum was sitting on the ground, his back leaning against the small house, munching on a raw ear of sweet corn.

Not wanting to frighten him, I called out softly, "Hey, Poudlum."

He looked up and said, "I was scared you wouldn't come, but you is right on time."

I slid down next to him and asked, "Y'all got much cotton in your house?"

"'Most a bale. You wants to let's jump in it some?"

Diving, jumping and falling into a huge pile of loose cotton was almost as much fun as sliding down the sawdust pile. It had been a whole year since I had done it, and I was sorely tempted. "Yeah, but what if somebody sees us?"

"Nobody to see us."

"Where's your family?"

"Dey all gone over to de river catfishing."

"How did you get out of going?"

"Told 'em it was too far to walk."

"We think alike, Poudlum."

"Huh?"

"Never mind, let's go jump in that cotton."

We romped, tussled, and frolicked until we lay breathless on the soft fluffy cotton. When we had rested a bit, I asked, "How long will it take us to get to that still?"

"Take a good half hour."

"How do we go?"

"Through de woods till we reach de Mill Creek, den just go straight down until it runs into de Satilfa."

It was true that if you went east on Center Point Road you would cross both streams, which were flowing south, but from there they both took sharp turns to the west and eventually merged. The Satilfa continued on to empty into the Tombigbee River.

"Let's get moving," I said. As we walked through the big stand of timber, I remembered what Jake had said about how many magnificent trees were here. I wondered why the Robinsons didn't sell some of them.

When we reached the stream Poudlum said, "Now, all we gots to do is wade down de creek a ways."

The creekbed made for easy walking because it had a

soft sandy bottom and the deepest it ever got was mid-calf. The treetops formed a canopy so it seemed as if we were wading through a tunnel in the forest.

When the creek was wide enough we walked side-by-side, otherwise Poudlum led the way. While we were walking along a wide part, I asked, "How come you were down here the first time?"

"I just wanted to see where dis creek went to."

"We got much farther to go?"

"Not too far—better to quit talking out loud," Poudlum said, his last few words diminishing into a whisper.

The creek widened and soon I could see a large expanse of water ahead. That's when Poudlum stopped, looked directly at me, put his forefinger to his lips and whispered, "Dat be de Satilfa—be real quiet and follow me."

He turned left and we entered the woods which covered the point-shaped strip of land between where the two streams became one.

After a few steps Poudlum dropped to his hands and knees, motioning for me to do the same. We crawled through the low undergrowth until we were on a high bank overlooking the Satilfa, well hidden in the thicket.

As we stretched out on our bellies and gazed toward the opposite bank I uttered a small gasp and whispered, "You sure didn't lie, Poudlum."

"Whisper real low 'cause sounds be easier to hear across water," he warned.

"How come?"

"I don't know, just does."

"What time was it when you were here before?"

"'Bout dis time."

"What did you do?"

"Same thing we be doing now."

"Let's just lay here for a while and see what happens. Maybe he comes here every Sunday afternoon to pick up his whiskey."

It was real quiet in those woods. The only sound was the burbling of the creek. The Satilfa was wide and deep enough here that you would have to swim it, so I knew that even if we were detected, we could make our getaway before anyone could get across. My eyes soaked in the scene on the opposite bank. There was a cleared area with what I guessed was all the necessities for making moonshine. I supposed that whoever worked it did it during the week, took Saturday off, and Old Man Creel picked it up on Sundays.

There was a big pot, some little pots with shiny copper pipes connecting them, and what looked like a truck radiator. Gallon jugs, buckets, and bottles were strewn about, and on a makeshift table in front of a shed, lay several funnels. Under the table were four heavy cardboard boxes.

The shed didn't have a front and I could see clearly inside it. There were more cardboard boxes and stacks of what looked like sacks of something. "What do you think is in those big sacks in the shed?" I whispered softly to Poudlum.

"Probably sugar and corn. I heard tell you gots to have both of dem to make shine," he whispered back.

We lay still for a long time while nothing happened. Finally I started getting restless because of the aggravating cramps and occasional itching. "Maybe we ought to swim over there and get a close look."

"Can't swim," Poudlum whispered back.

"Well, I sure as heck ain't gonna swim over there by myself."

"Don't have to swim."

"Course you would—that water's deep."

"Dey's a big tree blowed down a ways up de creek. You can walk all de way 'cross on it."

"How far?"

"'Bout a minute."

"Come on, let's go," I whispered.

But just as we rose to our knees, we heard the smooth purring sound of an automobile engine. It was him!

We froze, then slid back down into our former position. Glancing at Poudlum, I saw that his eyes were big. The engine went silent and a moment later we heard the slamming of a car door, then heavy footsteps crunching on the dry debris of the forest floor. Just be real quiet, I thought, and everything will be okay, then I had another frightening thought—what if he had that big bulldog with him?

Thankfully, he emerged from the mouth of the dim trail alone. Just like Poudlum had said, it was Old Man Cliff Creel, all right. Puffing on a cigar, he walked straight to the table, reached underneath it, and grabbed one of the boxes. After he set it on the table, he opened it, pulled out an amber-colored pint bottle, unscrewed the cap and took a long swig. "Yes sirree, mighty fine," he said to himself and licked his lips.

We watched while he disappeared back into the woods carrying one of the boxes. After he had made three trips, he came back huffing and puffing. But before he left with the fourth box, he reached into his coat pocket, pulled out a fat envelope, walked over to the hollow tree next to the shed, and stuffed the envelope in. Next, he grabbed a handful of dead leaves and stuffed them into the tree to cover the envelope.

We watched him leave with the last box of whiskey, heard the car door slam, the engine start, and the sound of it fade in the distance.

Simultaneously, Poudlum and I breathed big sighs of relief. "Poudlum," I asked, "did he do the same thing when you saw him before?"

"Huh?"

"Did he stick something in that hollow tree?"

"I don't know—I scooted right on out of here soon as I saw him take a bottle of whiskey out of one of dem boxes."

"Come on. Show me where that dead tree is that'll take us across the creek!"

10

The Money Tree

We crossed the fallen tree and crept out of the woods surrounding the still. "Don't touch anything, Poudlum. We don't want 'em to know we been here," I whispered.

"I ain't touching nothing—don't even want to be here."

"Won't take long—come on, let's see what's in that shed."

The big sacks were just as Poudlum had thought, sugar and corn. There were also several smaller sacks of yeast and a large supply of the boxes like the ones we had watched Old Man Creel tote away. I peeked inside one of the boxes and saw that it contained empty pint bottles. I quickly counted forty-eight and thought, no wonder he was breathing so hard—that had to have been a heavy load with them being full.

Now for the best part. I meant to see what he had stuffed into that tree. I stepped away from the shed and started toward the hollow tree when I heard Poudlum say in a loud hissing whisper, "Come on, let's get outta here!"

"Just gimme a minute," I said while I started digging the leaves out of the hole in the tree. To my sorrow, when I pulled the envelope out, it was sealed. I realized they would be onto us if I opened it, but I felt all around it, putting a little pressure around the edges, and knew in my heart that it was stuffed full of folding money, a lot of it. For a fleeting moment I wanted to take the whole thing, but thought no, not now. I put it back, along with the leaves. I was thinking, somebody makes this whiskey during the week, then on Sunday afternoons Old Man Creel picks it up and leaves their pay in the hollow tree.

There was only one other question in my mind: how did he drive his car back in here? "We got to see how he gets in here," I told Poudlum as I started toward the trail Old Man Creel had used.

"I ain't going in dem woods."

"Then wait here for a minute. I'll be right back."

"Uh-uh, I ain't waiting here by myself. You promise we'll leave if I come?"

"Promise. Now, come on."

It was just a short distance through the woods before we came on the end of an old logging road with a turn-a-round big enough for a car. I could see where the timber had been clear-cut all along the logging road and the new growth of pines and small hardwoods was only several years old.

"Where you think it goes?" Poudlum asked.

"It has to lead to Center Point Road on the other side of the Satilfa Creek bridge, because he couldn't drive his car across the creek. I'll find out this coming Saturday."

"How you gon' do dat?"

"While I'm on my paper route I'll cross the bridge, find the first old logging road on the right, then just follow it and see if it brings me here. Now, I'm ready to go."

When we got back to the Mill Creek, we ran all the way up it. At the cotton house, before we said good-bye, Poudlum and I promised each other that we would keep our secret until such time as we both agreed to tell anyone else.

Heading home, I stuck to the edge of the woods, just keeping Center Point Road in sight. I had my stick, but I didn't want to have to use it on that mean dog. I found myself thinking about what Poudlum said just as I was leaving: "I'll see you in de cotton field tomorrow when we be picking together."

I knew we wouldn't really be together because the colored hands would be on one side of the field and the white hands would be on the other. That bothered me, though I couldn't say exactly why.

But right now I was concerned about getting home before Fred, otherwise I would have to make up a story about where I had been. I knew he would have stopped at Miss Lena's if he was ahead of me. I decided to go into the store and ask, then if he was ahead of me I could use the time while walking on home to think up an explanation.

When I got to the store I went straight to the big red drink box and pulled out a cold Nehi. When I placed my nickel on the counter I said, "Hey, Miss Lena. You seen Fred?"

I didn't know much about Miss Lena, just that she

didn't have a husband and she was way past the age when she should've gotten one. She had a stout build and always had her hair stacked on top of her head. She did have a car, which she drove to the store everyday from wherever she lived—down near Coffeeville somewhere. No one ever said she was pretty, and I wasn't inclined to argue the point, but she always seemed to be in a good mood. Today she smiled down at me when she answered, "No, I haven't seen hide nor hair of that boy."

Then she reached into the penny cookie jar and gave me one for free. "Thank you, Miss Lena," I said on my way out.

I really wanted to stop and talk to Jake but I knew I didn't have time, so I walked fast all the way to the little road leading to our house. I stopped there and waited for Fred.

It wasn't long before I saw him coming down the little hill. "What you doing? he asked suspiciously when he got to where I was sitting with my back leaned against a tree.

"Waiting for you."

"What did you do all afternoon?"

"I just been playing, then I went to Miss Lena's and got me a drink." There, I thought, I had successfully avoided telling another lie.

He studied me a few moments, then I was relieved when he said, "Let's go see what's on the stove. I'm starving."

RIGHT AFTER SUPPER another thunderstorm came roaring in. Once it passed, the clouds stayed and it got dark early. We were all sitting around the kitchen table bathed in the glow of the dim light from the kerosene lamp—the only light we had after dark. I watched my father roll himself a cigarette. He held a flimsy rolling paper folded between his left thumb and middle finger, with the tip of his forefinger stuck just inside the fold to keep it open. From a cloth bag of Bull Durham tobacco he dumped a mound of the loose contents into the fold of the paper. The tobacco looked like sawdust to me. He spread it out, then with both thumbs and forefingers he rolled the paper tight and smooth, licked the seam, and popped it into his mouth.

Then he lifted the glass globe off the lamp, leaned forward until the tip of the cigarette touched the flame from the wick, and inhaled deeply until the tip turned bright red.

I knew from experience that the glass globe was hot but he could get away with handling it because his hands were so rough and calloused. During the winter he would pick up hot coals out of the fireplace with his fingers to light his smokes. I watched the curls of blue smoke drift up and disappear into the rafters.

Across the table my mother was attaching shoulder straps to our cotton-picking sacks. I became alarmed when she folded two ten-pound sacks, placed them on the table and said, "There, that's done."

"But that's only two!" I said, thinking I wasn't going to get to pick after all.

"There's one for you and one for Fred. I'll be busy canning and Ned will be helping your Uncle Curtis and Robert deliver a load of watermelons to Grove Hill."

I was relieved and I was also sleepy. The flickering of the lamp increased my drowsiness, making my head feel heavy. I placed it across my arms on top of the table and listened as the conversation of my family became a soft blur coming from somewhere far away. I barely remembered Ned half carrying me to bed. That night, I dreamed of great expansive fields of soft, white, downy cotton.

11

The Cotton Field

When I woke up I thought it was the middle of the night because it was still dark, but then I heard my mother's voice coming from the foot of the bed saying, "Y'all get up. Breakfast is on the table and your Uncle Curvin will be here before you know it."

Uncle Curvin had never been married and he still lived at Pa Will's house. He was partially crippled from being shot in the leg during the war, but he got around fairly well with a walking cane. Besides a disability check he got from the government, he made his living by growing a cotton crop every year. I had heard my mother say Uncle Curvin usually delivered about ten bales to the cotton gin each year, and that after paying for the chopping, the picking, and Old Man Cliff Creel, he would make himself about five hundred dollars. That seemed like a vast fortune to me.

Fred and I were waiting outside, right after first light, when we saw Uncle Curvin's old truck come rumbling toward the house. The truck bed had high wooden rails to hold the cotton in place. As soon as Uncle Curvin made a u-turn in the yard Fred began scampering up the rails to join several of our cousins and neighbors, all ranging from my age to their late teens.

I saw that Uncle Curvin was by himself in the cab, so I opened the door, jumped in beside him and said, "Hey, Uncle Curvin."

He was wearing a pair of overalls, a blue work shirt, and a straw hat with a piece of green-tinted plastic built into the front of the brim. There were deep creases in his face and his mouth was all caved in because he didn't have any teeth.

"Hey, little buddy," he replied. "You ready to pick some cotton?"

"Yes, sir. How much you think I can pick this week?"

"If you work real hard and don't be playing around a lot, like I know half them young 'uns on the back of the truck will be, you could pick twenty-five pounds a day. If you do that, then come Friday, you would have made a dollar and a quarter."

"Aw, I can pick more than that."

"We'll see."

"Can I ride with you to pick up the Robinsons?"

"Done picked them up. They already in the field picking."

"How come you went and got them first?"

"'Cause I need my cotton picked, and them folks are serious cotton pickers."

"How much will they pick this week?"

"They'll probably pick seven or eight bales."

"How many pounds in a bale?"

"Five hundred pounds to a bale. The old man and the

old woman will each pick two hundred pounds a day, and between their young 'uns, they'll pick another three hundred or more."

"How come they pick so much?"

"Lots of reasons: They just know how to pick, had lots of experience, and most importantly, they need the money."

"But they got their own cotton to pick."

"Yeah, they do. There's a full moon this week. I expect they'll be picking at night, then when I get my field picked, they'll have time to finish picking their own."

"How do they get their cotton to the gin?"

"Oh, I haul it for them after I haul mine."

"What do they do to the cotton at the gin?"

"Did you wake up with a question mark over your head this morning?"

"No, sir, I just wondered."

"The gin separates the fiber from the seed before the cotton is shipped off to the textile mills."

"Where did the gin come from?"

We were halfway up the big hill when my uncle had to depress the clutch and shift into a lower gear. Once he had the truck grinding on up the hill he said, "The gin was invented by a Connecticut Yankee named Eli Whitney."

"You mean to tell me a Yankee invented the cotton gin."

"I am sorry to report, little buddy, that is indeed the truth. However, he did it while he was over on the coast of Georgia, near Savannah."

"When did he do that?"

"He did it about a hundred and fifty years ago, and

I ain't answering no more questions," Uncle Curvin said when we turned onto Center Point Road. "You got your pick sack?"

"Yes, sir," I said, shaking it loose and showing it to him.

THE TRUCK LURCHED to a stop at the edge of the cotton field and everybody came tumbling off the back. Uncle Curvin got out, limped around to the back and said, "Listen up, everybody. Grab a row and start picking. There's empty sacks in the cotton house on the back side of the field, so when you fill your pick sacks you can empty it into one of them. Be sure and keep 'em separate so there won't be no arguing when I weigh 'em up at the end of the day. At that time I'll be checking for rocks. First sack I find with any rocks in it, then whoever it belongs to can get out of my field."

I figured his last remark was directed at Fred because he was always hiding rocks in his sack to make it weigh more. Uncle Curvin continued, "I don't want nobody messing with them darkies on the other side of the field, 'cause unlike most of y'all, they come here to work. I'll be back here in two or three hours with some cool water. Now, get to picking."

Fred quickly tied our brown paper lunch bag up high on a fence post to keep it away from the ants. It contained biscuits and smoked sausage left over from breakfast. Then he motioned me to follow him and we picked two rows next to each other and began pulling the cotton out of the bolls and stuffing it into our sacks. At first it was fun, being around so many people and listening to the talk and the laughter, but soon everyone had left me behind and I could barely hear them. Fred doubled back picking on my row and helped me catch up, but before long I was behind again.

I gave up trying to stay up with everybody, concentrated on just picking cotton, and soon discovered that it wasn't fun anymore, that it was actually back-breaking work. But I kept at it. Looking down the row I saw that the others had finished their rows and were emptying their sacks into the bigger sacks in the cotton house. I stood up on my toes and peered across the field. In the distance I could see the Robinsons picking away, with several bare rows beyond them which they had already stripped clean. I was amazed at how much cotton they had already picked.

Now everyone was coming back toward me, starting on their second row, and then for a while I was back in among the talking and the laughter. Eventually though, they were gone again and I was picking alone by the time I reached the end of my first row.

I turned and watched everyone getting further and further away. That's when I realized this day was going to be a lot longer than I had anticipated. I found one of the big empty sacks at the cotton house, emptied my sack into it, marked my spot, and was just about to head back toward starting my second row when I spotted Poudlum.

The top of his straw hat was just visible above the rows of white cotton. Then I noticed that no one was with him, that he was picking by himself, too. That's when I understood that the same thing was happening to both of us—because we were the smallest, we were being left behind.

I asked myself, why should we have to pick alone when

we could be picking together? I made my decision and started walking toward the other side of the field where I was going to be picking with Poudlum.

In the summer of 1948, I reverse integrated the cotton field.

POUDLUM WAS IN the middle of a row by himself when I caught up with him and I saw his eyes light up when I asked, "You want to let's pick together, Poudlum?"

"Sho does, I hates picking by myself. Just start in de middle of dis row next to me. We'll pick from de same row coming back, den split up when we gets back to where you started."

We started right off picking. "You ain't talked to nobody about yesterday, have you?"

"Naw, I ain't said nothing to nobody, has you?"

"No, and let's be sure and keep it that way, at least for right now."

It didn't take me long to notice that even though we were the same size, Poudlum kept getting ahead of me and had to slow down for me to catch up. This prompted me to ask, "How come you can pick so much faster than me?"

"One thing, you need to pick with both hands."

"Huh?"

"I noticed you holds de boll wid yo' left hand and pulls the cotton out wid yo' right. No need to hold de boll, just pull cotton out of separate bolls wid each hand. You only needs to hold de boll if it breaks off de stalk, and dat won't happen much."

I tried this for a while and sure enough it worked. I was

picking faster. "What else do I need to do?"

"Get yo' self a rhythm."

"How do I do that?"

"Don't just stand stiff, reaching wid only yo' hands and arms. Lean and sway all around de plant and let yo' hands fly."

Pretty soon I was almost able to keep up with Poudlum. "Anything else you can think of?"

"Find de fastest speed you can pick at and den stick wid it."

I put Poudlum's advice to practice and soon cotton was flying into my sack. Before long we passed his family going in the opposite direction. They all grinned and nodded while they kept picking.

When we reached the end of our row we took a small break to pack the cotton down into our sacks. Poudlum looked toward the road and said, "I wish yo' Uncle Curvin would hurry up wid dat water. I sho is thirsty."

We had only picked a few feet down our new row when we saw his truck pulling in on the other side of the field. I watched the people over there drop their sacks in the fields and start walking towards the truck. I guess they were thirsty, too. I turned my back toward them, resumed picking , and reassured Poudlum by saying, "It won't be long now."

In a few moments I noticed Poudlum had stopped picking. "Uh-oh," he said.

"What's the matter?"

"Look over dere."

I turned and saw several of the white pickers gathered around the truck, pointing straight toward Poudlum and me. Uncle Curvin was looking right at us, too.

After they had taken several gallon jugs of water off the truck, Uncle Curvin drove along the edge of the field towards us. When he stopped at the end of our row, Poudlum said, "He looks like he be mad."

"I don't know what about. Come on, let's get some water," I said while slipping the strap of the sack over my head and dropping it.

Uncle Curvin was out of the truck and limping around it when I said, "Glad to see you, Uncle Curvin, 'cause we are awful—"

"Boy, what did I say this morning about coming over here and bothering these folks? Now, get your sack and get on back on the other side of the field before I take a cotton stalk to you."

He did sound angry, and I was stunned. While I stood there with my mouth open he yelled, "You hear me, boy!"

"But I just come over here to pick with Poudlum 'cause can't neither one of us keep up with—"

"I don't care why you come over here. If you don't get—"

It was his turn to be interrupted, and it was by Mrs. Robinson as she came crashing across several rows of cotton. "Mister Curvin, dat child ain't bothering nobody on dis side of de field. Fact is, it be a pleasure to have him over here. Ain't nary thing wrong wid him and my Poudlum picking together."

Uncle Curvin wasn't intimidated. "He can get to the other side or get outta my field."

Mrs. Robinson wasn't intimidated either. She put her

hands on her hips and said, "Mister Curvin, if Mister Ted gots to leave den we does, too."

I could see the uncertainty on Uncle Curvin's face. "But it just ain't right for him to be over here with—"

"I'll take my whole family right out dis field."

His uncertainty changed to panic, then a defeated look appeared on his face. He let out a long sigh and said, "All right then, y'all come on and get some water. I know you're thirsty."

After Uncle Curvin was gone, we drank our fill of water, then stored the jugs next to the fence under the shade of some bushes.

When we headed back toward our cotton sacks, I looked at Poudlum's mother and said, "Thank you, Mrs. Robinson."

She stopped, looked down at me, and said, "I be de one who should be thanking you."

"What for?"

"'Cause on account of you my children got milk to drink, but more important dan dat, you de first white person to ever call me Misses."

Lunchtime presented a new dilemma. The Robinsons gathered around the shade with the water jugs where Mrs. Robinson produced two gallon syrup buckets. After popping the lids off she began passing out biscuits—big ones. A lot bigger than the ones my mother made. "You welcome to have a biscuit wid us, Mister Ted. We got plenty."

I wanted to go see Fred and eat with him, but I didn't want to offend the Robinsons. I decided to do both. The biscuit had a big fried slice of streak-o-lean in it. After I finished it I told Poudlum, "I'm going over to the other side of the field and see my brother. I'll be back in a little while."

I found Fred sitting alone in the shade of Uncle Curvin's truck with his back against the tire. I knew he had been in a fight when I saw his mouth. I asked, "How did you get a busted lip?"

"Got in two fights."

"How come?"

"On account of you."

"Why?"

"'Cause some of them are calling you a nigger-lover."

"But I just went over there to pick with Poudlum 'cause y'all were leaving me by myself."

"I know. Uncle Curvin came back and told everybody that. Everybody's okay now."

"I'm sorry you got hit in the mouth."

"It's all right. I busted them upside their heads good. They won't bother me no more. Here's your two sausage and biscuits. I already ate mine."

I took the paper bag and said, "I don't want but one. You eat the other one."

"You sure?"

"Yeah, eat it."

While we finished our lunch I told him everything Poudlum had taught me about picking cotton.

"So that's why they can pick so much more than us. I'm gonna try it and I ain't telling none of the others."

"I got to go," I said.

"I'll see you at the cotton house when we weigh up. See

if you can find out any more picking tricks," Fred said.

There wasn't a cloud in the sky that afternoon and the hot sun beamed down relentlessly. I was shirtless, but I didn't burn because I had been exposed to the sun all summer long. It was the sweat that bothered me. It would run down into my eyes and down my neck, and it burned. I noticed that Poudlum had a big rag in his pocket to mop his face and neck. I would remember that tomorrow.

Uncle Curvin made three more water deliveries and we guzzled huge amounts at the end of each row.

About midafternoon the ground became so hot I couldn't stand on it with my bare feet. Poudlum taught me to scrape away the first two inches of dirt and then stand in the spot we had excavated. The ground was cooler underneath the crust, so we kicked away the hot surface of the ground next to each plant as we approached it, then just kept picking.

I stood up straight—slowly because of my aching back— and looked toward the other side of the field. Only one lone figure was picking over there. It was Fred. The rest were piled up under a shade tree.

"You gots to get yo' self a straw hat so de sun don't bake yo' head," Poudlum said.

I looked down the row as the rest of his family approached us from the opposite direction and saw that they all had straw hats. I added "straw hat" to my list for tomorrow.

The next thing I knew, Fred came walking up to us, moving fast across the hot ground. "Poudlum," I said, "This is my brother, Fred."

"Hey, Mister Fred."

"Hey, Poudlum. I came over here to see how y'all bear to stand on the hot ground—"

He stopped talking because his eyes had lowered to the ground, then he said, "Oh, I see. Y'all just dig a hole and stand in it. I can do that. See y'all later." He took off back across the field.

"How old yo' brother be?" Poudlum asked.

"He's thirteen."

"He sho is big."

"Yeah, he's real strong too. And he can shoot marbles better than anybody."

"His hair is 'most white, just like you. My momma calls y'all de golden boys."

WE WENT BACK to picking and later on I found myself wondering how anybody could stand the torture any longer. That's when I heard the haunting sound coming from Poudlum's approaching family. It was almost as startling as when I first heard Jake singing the blues. I stared toward them. "What are they doing?" I asked Poudlum.

"Dey's singing."

"I can hear that, but why are they doing it out here in the middle of this cotton field?"

"'Cause sometimes when things get so bad you can't hardly stand it, den a little singing will take yo' mind to a finer place while yo' body stays and endures the pain."

"How you know all that, Poudlum?"

"'Cause my momma told me so."

"Well, I sure would like to be in a finer place. You think it'll work for us?"

"Sho it will—just listen."

It was true. The sound of their voices and the impact of the words made me forget the heat, the aches and pains, the thirst, and all the other discomforts. I kept picking cotton while the sweet words of the old spiritual swept over me.

"Nobody knows the trouble I've seen

"Nobody knows my sorrow . . ."

The effect of the singing stayed with me long after the sounds had faded, and the lesson of listening to it, letting it take you away, was forever embedded in my mind. I knew now that I could endure most anything by diverting my thoughts to something pleasant. I spent the remainder of the day thinking about the cool water of the Mill Creek, the taste of a peach Nehi, and many other happy thoughts while my body suffered. Before I knew it the day was over.

I saw Uncle Curvin's truck traveling along the edge of the field, then he came to a stop at the cotton house. I watched while he limped from the truck to the corner of the cotton house and hung the scale on a piece of wire dangling from one of the rafters. Then he turned toward the field and waved for everyone to come on in.

The cotton scale consisted of a long metal bar with two metal hooks on swivels about a third of the way down the bar. One hook was on top and one was underneath. The top one was what Uncle Curvin hooked to the piece of wire.

The cotton sack to be weighed was hung from the bottom hook, then the number of pounds it contained was determined by hanging weights onto the numbered notches on the bar until it became level.

Everybody had emptied their picking sacks into their

larger sacks and was dragging them toward the cotton house. The white pickers arrived first, except for Fred, who came straggling up when Poudlum and I did. The rest of the Robinsons were far behind because they had so many more sacks to drag up.

As Uncle Curvin weighed up one of the white pickers' sacks after another and passed out the coins, he said, "I know all y'all are gonna walk down to Miss Lena's store and spend every nickel you made today, so when I finish up I'll be taking the Robinsons home first, then I'll come and pick everybody up at the store and you'll all be home by supper time."

Then he got to Fred's sack.

Uncle Curvin moved the weights down the scale. When he reached fifty-five pounds, the scale finally balanced. It was the heaviest sack from that side of the field. He tinkered some with the scale, then looked sternly at Fred and said, "What did I tell you about putting rocks in your sack, boy?"

"Ain't no rocks in there, Uncle Curvin."

"Well, we'll just see about that," Uncle Curvin said. He turned the sack upside down and emptied it on the ground. Then he spread the cotton out and ran his fingers all though it, but he found no rocks.

"See," Fred told him.

"I can't believe you picked that much, but I guess you did. Put it back in the sack and I'll pay you."

Fred was stubborn. "I done put it in the sack one time. You emptied it, you put it back."

"Boy, I'll whack you with my walking stick if I have to. You pick up that—"

"We'll get it, Uncle Curvin," I said, tugging on Poudlum's arm. "Help me, Poudlum."

We stuffed Fred's cotton back into his sack while he glared at Uncle Curvin with his hand held out for his money.

Uncle Curvin questioned my sack, too, when it weighed in at forty pounds, but he paid me my forty cents, looked at us both, and said, "I'm sorry I questioned your weight, boys. I underestimated you. You both did a good job today."

"You wanna go to the store?" I asked Fred.

"Naw, let's save our money and just go on home. I'm tired and I'm hungry."

We cut across the field, climbed the fence, and were already halfway home when we reached Friendship Road.

I left that cotton field a lot smarter than when I had arrived that morning. Fred did, too. But more importantly, after integrating it, I had been a part of the first local threat of a boycott.

12

Fire

By Wednesday all the white pickers had abandoned the cotton field except Fred and me. On Thursday Fred moved over to the side of the field where the Robinsons and I were picking. We continued to amaze Uncle Curvin with the number of pounds we turned in at each weighing, but we were both glad when the end of the day came on Friday. We had proved ourselves capable in the cotton field, but there was only a day's work left before the field would be picked clean, and the Robinsons would complete that tomorrow. I had papers to sell and Fred had marbles to shoot, so we said good-bye to that cotton patch and went to Miss Lena's store for Nehis and MoonPies.

On Saturday, I had already completed the eastern part of my paper route well before noon, but instead of turning back west I continued east on Center Point Road. Pretty soon I saw the Saltifa Creek bridge up ahead. Before crossing it I stopped and listened hard for a car coming in either direction, because I knew that once I got in the middle of the bridge there would be no place to hide. Everything was so quiet I could hear myself breathing, so I trotted across, then started walking in the ditch on the right side of the road. Somewhere, not far, I knew there had to be an old logging road going into the woods.

I kept walking, ready to dart into the woods if I heard a car approaching. Not even a quarter of a mile past the bridge, there it was, with a big NO TRESPASSING sign nailed to a tree. I knew what that sign meant, but I paid it no mind.

After finding fresh car tracks I felt confident that this road led to the still. I started jogging because I knew it was a long way. What if the bootlegger came here on Saturdays? There were plenty of places to hide on either side of the road.

After a while I knew I was on the correct road because occasionally I could hear the Satilfa rippling off to the right. Suddenly, I came to the end of the road and knew the still was right through the woods ahead.

It was quiet and deserted. Everything looked the same, except there were six boxes instead of four under the table. Lifting the lid of the top one, I saw that they were full of whiskey, ready to be picked up. I counted forty-eight pint bottles inside the box.

Next I checked the hollow tree. It was empty but I figured it would be stuffed full of money tomorrow afternoon. Now it was time to go, but not the same way because I thought I had figured out a short cut. If I was right, I could check on the still every Saturday, count the boxes under the table, then when the time was right, make my move. I would wait till there were at least six boxes before I would return on one Sunday soon and rob that money tree.

I walked up the bank of the creek to the tree bridge Poudlum had showed me. The tree had fallen from the side of the creek I was on, and the big roots which had ripped out of the ground stood jagged and broken all around its base. I had climbed up on the trunk and taken two steps when I saw the boat. It was a wooden fishing boat, kind of like the ones my father built, about ten feet long, and it was lodged in the branches of the tree near the far side of the creek.

Halfway across there were branches to hold onto and to maneuver around. Just a few feet farther and I could look directly down into the boat where it was caught between two branches that descended into the water. The boat was empty except for an oar and a coil of rope tied to the bow. It was also dry, which meant it was a good boat that had probably gotten away from someone somewhere up the creek and floated down here before snagging in the branches of the fallen tree.

At first I thought about taking my stick and pushing it loose so I could watch it float on down the creek. Then I had another thought. It was a good boat, probably worth ten or fifteen dollars. Why not hide it and save it like I did empty drink bottles?

I stretched out on my belly on the trunk of the tree, stuck my stick under the rope, and lifted it up until I could grab it with my other hand. Then I got up and crossed on over to the other bank, letting the slack out of the rope as I went. Once I got to the other side I walked up the bank a few steps, tugged on the rope until the boat came out from between the two limbs, then pulled it over toward me. When it was right up next to the bank I used my stick again to push it under the brushy top of the fallen tree. Once I got it hidden I took the rope and tied it up tightly to another limb.

Satisfied that I had it well hidden, I crossed the narrow strip of land and splashed into the Mill Creek. When I got to the part of the creek where Poudlum and I had entered and exited, I kept going. It made sense to me that if I went farther, then turned left through the woods I should come out behind the sawmill.

I GUESSED HOW much time had passed to figure out when to exit the creek. I knew how long it took me to walk up Center Point Road from the road leading to Poudlum's house to Miss Lena's. When I thought that much time had passed, I turned into the woods, marking my spot by breaking a low limb off a big sweet gum tree.

After a while I heard a low mournful sound floating through the woods. I stopped, turned my ear toward the sound, and listened carefully. When I recognized it I knew I was real close to the sawmill. It was Jake singing the blues. I didn't want to scare him by coming in behind him, so I circled around the edge of the woods and came in toward the sawmill from my normal route. He had stopped playing and singing, and was sitting on the makeshift bench opening a can of sardines with his pocket knife. A can of pork and beans, already opened, was on the bench next to him with the jagged tin lid bent backward. Next to the can was a dime box of saltine crackers.

As soon as I got close enough, without yelling, I called out, "Hey, Jake."

"Mister Ted, come on over here. I just about to have

myself a bite to eat. You cares to join me?"

I guessed it was about one o'clock, and I suddenly realized how hungry I was. "You sure you got enough?" I asked while I slid onto the opposite end of the bench.

"Got plenty. Even if I didn't, I'd always share what I has wid you," he said as he finished opening the flat can.

We ate the salty little fish right out of the can with our fingers, and we scooped the beans out of the other one with the crackers. It was a mighty tasty meal, especially since I was so hungry. When we finished, he walked over to the fire and threw the empty cans in.

"You burn those cans?"

"Yeah, it keeps the varmints away. I sees you still got yo' stick."

"Uh huh, I take it with me everywhere."

He walked back over and while reaching underneath the bench said, "Well how 'bout if I trade dis one to you fo' it?"

The stick he handed me was a beautiful piece of polished hickory, just the right length, with a hole drilled through the handle where a strip of leather had been threaded though and tied. The end was rounded off, then it tapered down toward the handle which was perfect for my hand. On further inspection, I found "Mister Ted" had been carved along the length of it. I handled it with awe. "Good Lord, Jake, this is a mighty fine stick. And it's for me?"

"Got yo' name on it, don't it? Ain't quite as heavy as yo' old one, but wid its shape and balance I figures you could swing it quick enough to bust a bad dog upside his head real good."

"Or bash a snake with it," I said as I stood and took a practice swing.

"Dat too."

"I could even hurt a person real bad with this stick."

"If need be, I s'pose you could. You wants to let's walk up to de store and gets us a cold drank?"

Jake got an RC Cola and I got a NuGrape, then we went outside and sat on the ground in the shade of the oak tree. I watched him drink half the bottle, then he said, "I seed Mister Creel's big new car go by a while ago."

"Which way was he going?"

"West, down toward his house."

I was aching to tell Jake about the still and that I knew who was the bootlegger, but no, not quite yet, I thought. But I did want to figure out how much money was being stuffed into that hollow tree, so I asked Jake, "How much does a pint of whiskey cost?'

He looked at me with a frown and asked, "Why you be wanting to know something like dat?"

"I just wondered how much it costs my daddy when he buys a bottle." Lying again, I thought.

"A pint of good liquor cost you three dollars."

Now that I had a number to figure with, I wanted to change the subject, so I said, "I been picking cotton all week."

"I knows. Heard you gots to be real good at it."

"How you know that?"

"I walked down to the Robinsons' and had supper wid 'em last night. Dey told me all about yo' big week in de cotton patch. Yo' brother, too."

"Picking cotton is hard. I had enough to last me a while."

"'Spect de Robinsons feel dat way, too. Dey gon' finish yo' uncle's patch today, but den dey gots to finish dere own."

"How long you think that's gonna take 'em?"

"Dey say about two weeks. In fact dey gots to finish by den."

"How come?"

"'Cause if dey don't pay de taxes on dere property in three weeks, den dey is gonna lose it."

"The house too?"

"Everything."

"How much are the taxes?"

"Hundred and fifty dollars."

"Hundred and fifty dollars! Where in the world are they gonna get that much money?"

"Cotton bringing seventy-five dollars a bale, and dey figures on having two bales. Dey got one already in dey cotton house. Looking like everything gon' be okay."

SUDDENLY JAKE JUMPED to his feet, ran around to the front of the store, pointed west, and shouted, "Oh my Lawd, look over yonder!"

I leapt up, ran around to join him, looked toward where he was pointing and saw black smoke boiling up into the clear blue sky.

"Dat smoke look like it coming from de Robinson place. Come on, we needs to gets up to Mister Curvin's cotton field fast!"

Jake was a lot faster than me. By the time I got up to

the field Jake and the Robinsons' were all on the back of Uncle Curvin's truck, and he was pulling it onto Center Point Road.

I jumped up on the running board on the passenger side, stuffed my stick and *Grit* bag through the open window, then dived through it into the cab with Uncle Curvin. He never said a word, just kept working the clutch and the gears until he had his old truck going as fast as it would go. We passed Miss Lena's store trailing a big red cloud of dust.

We slid sideways on the loose ground when Uncle Curvin turned off the main road. Then he topped the hill and the house and fields came into view and we saw that the cotton house was already burned to the ground with nothing left but a smoldering pile of ruined cotton. Even worse, the fire was roaring across the field heading straight toward the house with the wind behind it. I heard a chorus of moans from the back of the truck.

Uncle Curvin gunned the old truck and skidded to a stop in front of the house. He didn't waste any time. Got right out of his truck and started yelling orders. "All you young 'uns run as fast as you can to the woods and break the tops out of some small pine trees. Get two each and meet the rest of us in the middle of the field."

Poudlum, his brothers and sisters, and I all stood motionless for a moment, frozen in fear, until he harshly yelled, "Get your tails moving, now!"

We took off, running like deer. When we returned to the field with the pine tops I saw what my uncle had in mind. He, Jake, and Mr. and Mrs. Robinson had positioned themselves halfway between the fire line and the house, where they were racing down four rows of cotton pulling the plants out of the ground and throwing them in the direction of the advancing fire. They were making a fire break.

When we came running up behind them, Uncle Curvin turned and yelled, "Y'all spread out across the field, take them pine tops, and beat out any fire that crosses that line. As soon as we got to the end we'll come back and help y'all."

For the next two hours we raced around beating out small fires, helping each other when it became too much for one, choking and coughing, until finally nobody could find a spark anywhere.

Two of Poudlum's older brothers were dispatched to the tree line behind the burned-out cotton house to make sure the fire didn't spread into the woods.

By the time they returned to report their success, someone had drawn two buckets of fresh water from the well. Everyone sat or leaned on the edge of the porch while we passed the water around, silently celebrating our success, and at the same time looking glumly at the devastation. I wanted to stay and grieve with them, but Uncle Curvin made me get in the truck with him. I looked through the back glass as we were pulling away. Mrs. Robinson was sitting on the front porch steps with her face in her hands.

When we reached Center Point Road, I thought about Mrs. Annie Pearl and the others waiting on their *Grit* paper, but I just didn't have the heart or the strength to carry on. So when Uncle Curvin asked, "What you wanna do?" I told him I just wanted to go home.

"Okay, little buddy, I'll take you."

We passed Old Man Cliff Creel's house and I saw him

sitting in his front porch swing, sipping on what looked like a glass of iced tea. I'm going to get you, old man, I thought.

When we turned into the road to my house, Uncle Curvin reached over, tousled my hair, and said, "We did all we could, and you did real good."

I knew what the Robinsons were facing and who had caused it, and thought, no, I haven't done all I can do, not yet.

13

The Cotton Gin

My mother sent me straight to the wash tub when I got home. I hadn't realized that I was covered with soot from head to toe. Then after I had washed and changed she noticed that my hair was singed, so she sat me in a chair on the front porch where she proceeded to work on me with her clippers. She gave the haircuts at our house, and it wasn't a pleasant experience. Occasionally her clippers would pinch and they always left my neck feeling chafed. While I was suffering I listened to Uncle Curvin tell her about the fire. "It was touch and go for a while there, especially with the wind blowing, but we finally beat it out. If we had got there five minutes later, then the house would of been gone. At least we saved that."

"How about the cotton, did it all burn?"

"A good portion of it, but I 'spect they might have close to a bale left in the field to pick."

"Them poor folks. Curvin, you think somebody set that fire?"

"I don't know about nothing like that."

I did. I figured it was Old Man Creel, and that he had done it so the Robinsons couldn't sell their cotton and pay their property tax, but I didn't say a word.

I forgot about the pain of having my neck scraped when I heard Uncle Curvin say to my mother, "I'll be taking a load of cotton to the gin come Monday morning. You think it'll be all right if Ted rides along?"

"It's all right, if he wants to go."

"Yes, ma'am, I want to go. Uncle Curvin, can I ride on the back of the truck on top of the cotton?"

"Course you can."

"What time will we be leaving?"

"I'll be at the cotton house, loading up, about seven o'clock Monday morning. You be there."

I suffered through church services again the next morning, not listening to anything that preacher had to say. Fred had invented a new game. Just before we went inside he gave me an empty match box and three marbles, then he explained the rules. I could put any number of marbles into the box and put it on the pew between us, and he would signal with his fingers his guess of how many were inside. As long as he didn't guess the number, I got to keep the box, but once he did, it passed to him, then I would have to guess.

I was amazed at his ingenuity and decided he hated being in church as much as I did. Anyway, his game passed the time away and then we were outside watching everybody stand around in the churchyard talking.

I saw Old Man Creel moving around through the crowd, shaking hands, smiling his evil smile, and I just knew he was spreading his foul message. A little later I saw him drive the big station wagon out of the churchyard, and I wondered if anyone else had any notion where he was going. I knew that after he had dinner he was going to pick up a load of illegal whiskey, and I meant to find out what he did with it.

As usual, we all went on down to Uncle Curtis's house for Sunday dinner. He always had ice at his house. Twice a week the ice truck delivered a giant block. I had been there before and watched them deliver it. The truck had a covered body on the back, and inside were great blocks of ice covered with quilts to insulate and keep the ice from melting. The ice man would take a big pair of black tongs with pointed ends and handles on the top, snatch up the block, bring it inside, and deposit it into the ice box.

I also knew there would be fried chicken. Along with it we had fresh black-eyed peas with tender snaps, creamed potatoes, and roasted ears of corn. But there was a special treat today. Besides iced tea, there was a choice of orange or lime Kool-Aid. I looked at the pitchers and thought that the colors were as pretty to look at as it was sweet and tangy-tasting on my tongue.

After Sunday dinner was over, the grown-ups congregated on the back porch in rocking chairs and began shelling peas.

My cousin Robert announced that he was going to drive to Coffeeville, so I told my mother I was going to ride with him as far as Miss Lena's and go on home. But after he dropped me off I kept on walking west hugging the edge of the woods. I entered the woods at the same spot as last Saturday, eight days ago. I didn't plan on getting close enough for that bulldog to catch my scent today, because I didn't need to hear, I just wanted to see. I picked out a big loblolly pine tree with low limbs, easy for climbing, but bushy and rising above the surrounding ones.

I felt naked because my mother hadn't let me take my stick to church, so I searched around the ground until I found a substitute, then I began climbing.

Halfway up the tree I found a comfortable spot where I could wedge myself in between two fat limbs and lean back against the trunk. From there I had a clear view of the house, the yard, and all the outbuildings which belonged to Old Man Creel.

I guessed by the position of the sun that it was between two and three o'clock, about the time he ought to be picking up his whiskey. I knew I might be waiting for nothing, but I was just going to wait and see what happened.

To pass the time, I began to study the details of the property. Several cows were grazing in the pasture behind the barn. They were all red except one, which was white with black spots and had a cow bell around her neck that clinked as she moved about. I made a mental note to ask Poudlum what color their milk cow was, but I figured it was the black and white one.

A sudden motion got my attention back toward the house. An unfortunate chicken had wandered into the back yard and that mean dog had it in his massive jaws, shaking and crushing the life out of it. Once there was no life left in the bird, he settled down on the ground and began ripping it apart.

The dog munched on his Sunday chicken for a while,

then his head jerked and his ears stood straight up. I watched as he rose to his feet and started trotting around the house toward the front. Looking that way, I saw what he had heard. It was his master in his station wagon.

I suspected success when I saw the car backing into the carport rather than pulling in. Old Man Creel got out, came through the gate, patted his dog on its head, and started walking toward the smokehouse. He took a key and unlocked the padlock on the door, returned to the car, unlocked the trunk, and extracted one of the boxes. One of the very boxes I had seen under the table at the whiskey still yesterday. I watched as he transferred all six boxes from his car trunk to his smokehouse. Instead of keeping smoked meat, he apparently kept illegal whiskey.

Only after he had disappeared through the back door did I descend from my lookout spot.

During the walk home I began to contemplate what I was going to do with all the information I had discovered. By the time I got there I had decided that I was going to need some help. The only question was, who?

On Monday morning, dew was still on the ground and my feet had gotten wet walking across the cotton field. Last week it had been a fluffy white sea full of people, now it was gray and empty. My uncle's truck was backed up to the door of the cotton house and the bed was already half full. I found him inside stuffing cotton into a big round basket almost as tall as me. Another big basket was hanging on the wall.

"'Bout time you got here. Grab that other basket and start filling it up."

"Yes, sir."

After Uncle Curvin had emptied several more baskets into the back of the truck, he said, "I'll take care of the rest of the loading. I want you to climb up on top of the cotton in the truck and start jumping up and down all over it."

I didn't mind doing it; in fact anticipated it being a lot of fun, but I wondered why he wanted me to do that. While I was climbing up I asked, "How come you want me to do that?"

"Need to pack it down real good."

I still wasn't satisfied. "Why does it need to be packed down?"

"Two reasons: so I can get more on the truck, and so it won't blow off."

Uncle Curvin loaded and I packed until the truck was almost full. He dumped the last basket on my head and I was completely buried. When I dug my way out, I saw his toothless grin, then he said, "Pack the rest of that down good and we'll hit the road. Pays to get to the gin early or we'll be sitting in line."

When we pulled out of the field onto Center Point Road he stuck his head out of the window and yelled back at me, "We won't be going too fast, but hold on tight."

After we crossed the Satilfa Creek bridge, I saw the old logging road. I wondered if someone was down the creek making whiskey, and if so, who could it be. I meant to find out one day this week.

It was a grand ride, sitting atop all that cotton, and it lasted over an hour because Uncle Curvin only drove about twenty miles an hour.

I had never seen a cotton gin before and kept conjuring up images of what it might look like. Nothing I had brought to mind was even close. When we slowed and began pulling off the road there was a long line of trucks in front of us, all filled with cotton. I heard Uncle Curvin say, "Oh, Lordy, looks like we gonna be here a while."

The gin was the biggest structure I had ever seen, built entirely of tin with no windows. It had just one door that I could see, which seemed tiny compared to the building. On the far side of the gin I saw big rectangular bundles of cotton wrapped in burlap and bound with metal straps. Uncle Curvin had pulled into the line and killed the motor. When he got out of the truck I pointed toward the bundles and asked, "What're those things?"

"That's cotton that has been ginned and is ready to be shipped to the textile mills."

"That's what they do to the cotton inside there?"

"Yep. They got machines inside that remove the seeds and pack the cotton into those tight bundles. Each one's a bale—five hundred pounds."

"Good Lord," I said in wonder.

"I'm gonna walk up the line, talk to a few folks. You stay put. I'll be back in a minute."

Up at the front of the line, I saw an empty truck pull off a platform, then the next one, fully loaded, pulled onto the platform. Above the platform was an overhang attached to the building. The next thing I saw truly amazed me. A colored man climbed up onto the back of the truck, stood on the top of the cotton, reached up and grabbed a big pipe out of the overhang and put the opening of it down close to the cotton where it started sucking it straight up. He moved all around with the big sucking pipe, and in no time at all, the truck was empty.

Uncle Curvin came back and saw me looking. "You best get up here in the cab with me or you'll get sucked up that pipe with the cotton and shipped off to one of them mills, then before you know it you'll be a shirt."

When it was our turn I asked, "What's this platform we're driving onto?"

"It's a big pair of scales, They weigh the truck when we first get on it, weigh it again after the cotton's gone, subtract the second weight from the first, and that's how they'll know how much my cotton weighed."

"Oh."

After we were unloaded Uncle Curvin pulled his truck over next to a small building and said, "I got to go in the office and get my money. Be right back."

While he was gone I saw a fat man in a brown uniform, wearing a badge on his chest and a pistol on his waist, milling around talking to people. When my uncle came out of the office, the fat man called out, "Hey, Murphy. Wait up. I need to talk to you a minute."

I slid across to the driver's seat to make sure I could hear everything.

"How's your cotton crop?" the man asked.

"'Bout average. What can I do for you?" Uncle Curvin replied.

I could see the fat man up close now. One of his cheeks bulged with a big chew of tobacco and there were slime stains going down from the corners of his mouth. He turned his head, spat a dark stream, then said, "Looking for a nigger that busted out of a prison over in Georgia. Folks over there think he might be somewhere hereabouts. They tracked him to Greenville, then lost the trail."

"Why you asking me?"

"I'm asking everybody. Figured the gin was a good place to be asking around 'cause folks coming in here from all over the county. His name is Jake Johnson. You seen or heard of this boy?"

I couldn't believe what I was hearing, that Jake was an escaped convict.

"There was a darkie working down to the sawmill who just showed up two or three weeks ago."

"What's he look like?"

"Well—"

"I know, they all look alike. I want to thank you for yer help. I'll be riding down that way first thing tomorrow morning and check him out. Thanks again for yer time."

I GOT BACK on the other side of the cab before Uncle Curvin got to the truck. He revved up the engine and we took off. We rode in silence for a while, then I asked, "Who was that fat man with the pistol?"

"That was the county sheriff, Elroy Crowe."

"He a good sheriff?"

"Good for nothing."

"What you mean?"

"He's in cahoots with every bootlegger in the county. Takes payoffs from 'em and come election time he'll use the money to buy votes. Did you hear what he had to say?"

"Yeah. Why did you tell him about Jake?"

"Had to. If I had lied and then he comes and finds him, well, I would be in trouble then."

Once again, we rode in silence for a while, then Uncle Curvin said, "That's a mighty fine stick you got. Jake make it for you?"

"Yes, sir."

"You think a lot of him, don't you?"

"Yes, sir."

"He seems like a decent sort to me, too. If it hadn't been for his help everything the Robinsons have would have been ashes. I know you visit him down at the sawmill. Maybe you need to visit him again later today."

We stopped at a cafe where Uncle Curvin bought me a hamburger, the first one I had ever eaten. He just had a bowl of pot likker with cornbread, 'cause he didn't have any teeth.

It was about midafternoon when we got back to his cotton house and started loading the truck again. When we were just about through and the cotton house was almost empty Uncle Curvin said, "I'm gonna leave a pile of cotton and a few empty sacks in here. If somebody needed a place to hide and sleep for a while, then this cotton house would be ideal. And if that somebody could get to the Tombigbee and cross it just before dark, then they could make it to Waynesboro, Mississippi, by daylight. From there, a person can catch a Greyhound bus to most anywhere."

Just before he got into his truck he handed me two quarters and said, "Here's your pay for the day. I'm gonna take this load by myself. You just stay here at the cotton house until the sawmill shuts down for the day. You know what to do then, don't you?"

"Yes, sir." I said. Then I wrapped my arms around his waist and hugged him, because I loved him.

14

Hiding Out

I couldn't imagine Jake being in prison. Maybe it wasn't him they were looking for. I was just about to find out. I came out of the woods as soon as there was no one left at the sawmill except him. I saw him sitting on his bench taking his shoes off and I called out, "Jake, Jake, I need to talk to you."

"Sho, we can talk long as you wants to. Just let me get des old brogans off, 'cause my old dawgs needs to breathe a little."

"We might not have as much time as you think."

"Huh? What in de world has got you so flustered?"

I saw the fear flicker across his eyes when I asked, "Is your last name Johnson?"

"It is, but how you knows dat? I ain't told nobody round here my whole name."

"You got to get out of here, Jake! You got to get out of here tonight!"

By the time I finished telling him of the day's events

he had his shoes back on and a forlorn look on his face. "I done run so long and so far, but now I gots to start running again. Thought I had got 'em off my trail and I could rest a while, but naw, dey don't never quit. Guess I'll just get my stuff and start walking, maybe walk all night. I just be so scared dat somebody gon' see me crossing some field or some road and—"

"No, Jake, I didn't mean get out of the county. What I meant was that you need to get away from this sawmill, 'cause this is the first place that sheriff will come looking. Then when he don't find you here, he'll go looking in other places."

"What you gots in mind?"

"My Uncle Curvin's cotton house. You can hide out there until we figure things out."

Jake got a deep thoughtful look on his face and asked, "So you is saying dat instead of running I should just go across de road and hide in a cotton house?"

"Yeah. Go after it gets dark tonight."

"What about yo' Uncle Curvin?"

"He's the one who put the idea in my head. He even said he's going to leave some cotton and a few empty sacks in it."

"Cotton house ain't a bad place to sleep. I done it before. Dey won't 'spect me to be right here, 'cause dey gon' think I be running. Dey be driving all over the county looking fo' me."

"That's right, and you won't have to worry about food, 'cause I'll bring you some. Then when things quiet down, I think I know a way to get you out of the county without you ever having to cross a road or a field."

"You gon' be dangerous when you gets grown, smart as you is now. I be putting my trust in you, and I be moving across de road tonight."

"Good, take whatever food you have with you and I'll come by sometime tomorrow or the next day and bring you some more. The cotton house is in the back of the field so I can come to it through the woods without being seen. There's a branch behind it, just a little ways into the woods, so you'll have water. I got to go now, but I'll see you at the cotton house."

I had only taken a few steps when I heard Jake say, "Mister Ted, wait."

I turned and asked, "What?"

"I just hopes you don't think too bad of me now dat you knows where I come from. I didn't do nothing real bad, I swears I didn't."

"I know you didn't. I just know it. You still my friend, Jake. Will you tell me all about it?"

"Sho will. I see you across de road."

TUESDAY NIGHT AT supper I listened while my father was telling everyone what I already knew. "That nigger, Jake, been working at the sawmill turns out to be an escaped convict from over in Georgia."

My mother was walking around the table spooning second helpings of chicken-and-dumplings onto everybody's plates when she asked, "How'd you find that out?"

"That sorry Sheriff Crowe came by looking for him

this morning. Said he had busted out of prison in Jackson, Georgia, 'bout three months ago."

"Did he catch him?" she asked.

"He couldn't catch a rabbit with a pack of hounds. Jake wasn't nowhere to be seen this morning."

"You think he'll get away?" Momma asked while she refilled my plate.

"I hope so, 'cause we all liked Jake, but the sheriff said they'd be watching all the roads. This shore is mighty good chicken-and-dumplings."

Momma completed her trip around the table and sat back in her seat and helped her own plate. "Thank you. That old hen had quit laying, so there wasn't nothing else to do with her."

The chicken-and-dumplings was real good. I set about planning on getting some of it out of the house. After we finished supper everyone went in different directions. My mother went to nurture her garden, my father to work on his boat, while Fred went with Ned to check his bird traps. As soon as everybody was out of the house I took an empty quart fruit jar, filled it up, and left for Jake's hiding place.

A half-hour later, I called softly from the edge of the woods behind the cotton house, "Jake, you in there?"

I saw one of the big wide boards being pushed outward from the bottom, then Jake slid out through the opening and joined me in the woods. "I thought my nose was playing tricks on me, Mister Ted, but I see it didn't. Praise de Lawd, dat is chicken-and-dumplings you got."

He smacked his lips and sighed with satisfaction when he finished. "I'll go down to the branch and wash dis jar out, 'cause I know it belongs to yo' momma."

"No, you just keep it. She's got so many she can't keep up with 'em."

"Good, 'cause it will come in handy. I can use it to fetch some drinking water from the branch."

"How much food you got?"

"I gots enough canned stuff, potted meat, Vienna sausage, sardines, beans, and crackers to last me a week if need be. I gots a little money, too."

"That's good, 'cause it may be two weeks before we can get you outta here with everything you need. I'll bring you food when I can, and we'll buy some more if we have to."

"What you talking about? I don't want to stay cooped up in dis cotton house fo' two weeks."

"Well, maybe sooner, but I've got a plan and I got to have some help to make it work."

"Tell me what you gots in mind."

"I know who the bootlegger is, where he has his whiskey made, where he keeps it, where he hides his money, and I need you to help me figure out a way to see that he gets caught."

Jake's eyes grew wide. "Say what!"

I repeated myself. When it had sunk in asked, "Who is de bootlegger?"

"It's Old Man Cliff Creel!"

Jake's eyes widened again. "Dat don't surprise me none, but I don't know how I can help you see he gets caught. It ain't like I can go talk to the sheriff about it."

"Wouldn't do no good to talk to that sheriff anyway."

"Why not?"

I told him what Uncle Curvin had said about his re-
lationship with the bootleggers. "We got to find someone
else to get him."

All of a sudden Jake's eyes lit up. "Probably take a few
days, but I just might knows a way. You wait right here." I
watched him while he sneaked back into the cotton house,
then in a few moments he was back in the woods with a
pencil, a piece of paper, and an envelope. He settled down
on the ground, grasped the pencil in his hand and started
writing on the envelope.

"What you doing?"

"I be putting de address on dis envelope."

"Who you sending it to?"

"To de Alabama Beverage Control department up in
Montgomery, de capital city."

"Who're they?"

"Dey is de folks what works fo' de state whose job it is
to catch bootleggers, and dey be serious about it. Chances
are, dey won't be no folks working fo' dem who be crooked
like dat sheriff looking fo' me."

He finished the envelope, spread the sheet of paper out
in his lap, and began speaking the words as he wrote them.
"Gentlemen, dis be to inform you 'bout a bootlegger down
here in Clarke County by de name of— How you spell dat
old man's name?"

"I don't know. Just like it sounds, I guess."

Before he began laboring over the piece of paper again
he asked, "Where you want me to tell dem dat still is?"

"No, I don't want them to know that."

"How come?"

"'Cause that's where he leaves the money. He picks up the whiskey from the still, then hauls it over to his house and locks it up in the smokehouse."

"How you knows all dis?"

"'Cause when we first went to the still, we watched him carry the whiskey away, then—"

"Wait a minute. Did you say, we?"

"Yeah, me and Poudlum."

"Lawd, have mercy. Go on."

"Then this past Sunday, about the time I figured he'd be getting home, I climbed a tree so I could see all around his house. Sure enough, about midafternoon he brought all the whiskey home and put it in his smokehouse."

Jake began chuckling and said, "Dis be almost too good to be true." Then he began writing and speaking again. "Mister Creel, who lives on Center Point Road between Coffeeville and Miss Lena's sto—"

He stopped and asked, "What day is dis?"

"Today is Tuesday."

Jake looked off into space and began speaking as if to himself. "If we mail dis letter tomorrow, which will be Wednesday, den it ought to be delivered by Friday. If so, de state revenuers might just get here by Sunday. Den dat might be a good time for me to ease on out of here."

"What's a revenuer?"

"Uh, dey be de whiskey police. Now, let me finish dis letter." He leaned over with his pencil and continued: "Will have a large amount of moonshine whiskey locked up in his smokehouse sometime after three o'clock dis coming Sunday afternoon."

At this point, he stopped, looked out toward nowhere again and asked himself, "Now, how is I gonna finish it?" After a moment he said, "Okay, here's what I gonna say: We, de concerned citizens, certainly hopes you all will do yo' duty and enforce de law."

He looked up at me and asked, "How's dat?"

"That's real good. You think it'll work?"

"Worth a try."

"Where'd you learn to write a letter like that?"

"I learned my letters and my numbers in school. Finished de fifth grade, but learned most of my writing and reading in de—" He paused, then continued, "Since you already knows anyway, in de pen."

"You said you was gonna tell—"

"I know, I said I gon' tell you all about it, and I intends to, but first, let's finish dis letter writing business." He folded the piece of paper, then he stuffed it into the envelope, licked it, and pressed it closed.

"You want me to mail it?"

"Naw, somebody might see you put it in de mail box, den go post a piece of mail demselves, see our envelope and know you be sending it. Be getting dark fo' long and you gots to be getting home. Best if I sneak over dere real late tonight and put it in de box, 'cept I ain't got no stamp."

The mail boxes at the corner across from Miss Lena's store were shared by everyone in the vicinity, and I knew you didn't need a stamp. You could just leave your money stacked on your envelope and the mail rider would take it and affix a stamp. I fished around in my watch pocket, dug out three pennies, handed them to Jake and said, "You don't need one—just put these pennies on the envelope." I hated giving up my money, but it seemed like a small amount to invest since it was going to net me a tree full of money.

"What time does you got to be home?"

"It's okay as long as I get there before dark."

"Den I s'pose we gots time fo' my pitiful story, dat is, if you still wants to hear it."

I slid over next to a tree, leaned back against the trunk, pulled my knees up under my chin, and said, "I sure do. Tell me everything, way back from the beginning."

Jake took a deep breath and began: "I never had me much of no real family. Lived wid my Aunt Essie Mae since before I could remember, but she was on her own and had a passel of her own young 'uns, so when I was 'bout fifteen I lit out on my own. Worked all over South Carolina, Georgia, and parts of Florida, mostly picking crops. De trouble all started 'bout eight years ago when I was picking peaches over in middle Georgia. Besides picking, my job was to haul wagon loads of peaches up to de railroad stop fo' shipping, then, on my way back, I had to pick up groceries fo' de folks what owned the peach farm."

"During de trips I usually stopped fo' a drink of water at de house of a colored family named McDonald. Had dat grand old name, but dey was pore as dirt. On dis particular day, de only thing dey had to eat was some corn meal full of weevils and a hunk of salt pork. So later on, when I was transferring all dem boxes of fine food from de porch of de general store onto de wagon, I picked up an extra box. It had a big cured ham, flour, meal, lard and some canned goods in it."

"You took it to those poor folks, didn't you?"

"Sho did, but then the next day, de sheriff come looking fo' it. Said he wanted de box of groceries back dat I had picked up by mistake. Well, de folks dat I worked fo' told him dat dey hadn't seen no extra box, and I told him de same thing. But it seems dat somebody seed me do it, so de sheriff puts cuffs on my hands, irons on my feet, loaded me in de back of his car and hauls me off to de jail house."

"Why didn't you just tell him what you had done with them?"

"Couldn't, 'cause den he would've locked dem up for taking stolen stuff."

"What happened?"

"After a few weeks in dat jail, eating nothing but corn pone and fatback, dey give me a trial and sentenced me to ten years in de state pen."

"Just for taking some food and giving it to poor people?"

"Sho did. Next thing I know I wuz working on a chain gang."

"Did they feed you any better?"

"Yeah, instead of having fatback wid de thin yellow corn pone, we had white beans wid it."

"That's all?"

"Fo' dinner and supper it wuz. Fo' breakfast we had more corn pone wid blackstrap molasses. Dat wuz what we had six days a week, but on Sunday we had vegetables out of de garden we grew."

"I don't blame you for breaking out."

"Dis wuzn't de first time."

"You broke out before?"

"Busted out seven times, but dis is de only time I ever got clean away, so far, dat is. All my life I figured dat if you wuzn't in a place you wanted to be, den you oughts to leave. So I just kept leaving, but dey always caught me, up until now. Sometimes a day, sometimes a week, but me and all dey others always got caught."

"How did you manage to get away this time?"

"It was easy. I made myself a plan fo' after I busted out. Every time before I would plan how to get out, but I didn't plan what to do after dat. I would just run and run until dem dogs caught up wid me, and dey always did. But dis time was different. While I wuz out working on de roads I found everything I wuz gon' need, in de order I wuz gon' need it."

"What you mean?"

"I knowed where dere wuz a chopping block wid an ax to cut de chains between de irons on my legs—dat was my first stop. Knowed when dis lady's wash day wuz and what day clothes would be hanging on de line. Knowed what time de train would be coming by and where it would be going slow enough fo' me to jump on board. Figured out how to deal wid dem dogs too. I dried me some hot peppers from the prison garden, had 'em ground up real fine. When I changed out of dem prison clothes, I left 'em in a pile filled wid hot pepper. From my hiding place I seed 'em start ripping dem old clothes up, den dey started snorting, sneezing, and rubbing dey noses wid dey paws. Dat pepper killed dere sense of smell. A little ways farther I heard dat train whistle blow and I knew I wuz gon' make it."

We sat for a long time, neither of us saying a word. Finally, Jake said, "You best be getting on home fo' dark sets in."

I got to my feet and said, "Okay, but I'll be by sometime tomorrow, and don't you worry about nothing."

I had taken a few steps when Jake called out, "Mister Ted, you think you could bring me a few of your momma's dried hot peppers?"

15

The Whiskey Maker

Where you been?"

"Just playing," I told my mother.

"Well you get around back and wash your crusty feet before you get into bed."

"Yes, ma'am."

She was standing on the ground and had several brown paper bags lined along the edge of the porch, which she was filling with butter beans from a big basket next to her feet. The bags were old and limp and kept flopping over when she tried to put the beans in them. "Well, don't just stand there. Get over here and hold these bags open for me."

Besides us eating them and her canning them, she sold a lot of the vegetables from her garden. Her butter beans went for five cents a pound and were a favorite with everyone. Every year she dried some in the hull and saved them for seeds. She claimed they had been in the family for three generations. I held the bags open while she filled them, then she topped each one off to make them even. "There," she said, "That looks like five pounds in each bag. You want to deliver them for me?"

"Yes, ma'am."

"All right, you can take Mrs. Blossom her bag, and don't forget to get my quarter."

This was good news to me because now I didn't have to make up a story to get away from the house tomorrow.

"Can I go see if I can find somebody to shoot marbles with after I take 'em?"

"Long as you don't gamble with 'em. Now, go wash your feet."

Later on, while we lay in bed, Fred and I could hear the soft murmur of the conversation of our parents and Ned coming from the front porch. Though a breeze was coming through the open window, I was hot, sticky, and sweaty. "It's so hot I can't sleep," I whispered.

"Get up and come on—I can fix that."

"What you gonna do?"

He was already on his feet and standing at the window when he said, "Take the top sheet and pass it out the window to me after I'm outside."

I watched him disappear through the window, then I took the sheet over to it and looked outside. He was standing beside the rain barrel and said, "Throw the sheet out to me." I did, and I couldn't believe it when, in the moon light, I saw him stuff it into the rain barrel. He said, "Get on out here and help me."

When I got outside he drug the sopping wet sheet out of the barrel, handed me one end, took the other himself, and said, "Now twist."

We twisted and twisted that sheet until instead of sopping wet, it was just damp, then Fred tossed it back through the window and said, "Come on, let's climb back in."

When we were back inside he said, "Now, get in the bed."

I did and he furled the damp sheet out and jumped under it with me before it settled down on top of us. "Now just wait," he said.

I lay there for a few moments, then the breeze from the open window started fluttering the damp sheet over our bodies. A few more minutes and I had goose bumps; in fact, later in the night I exchanged the sheet for a warm quilt. My brother had introduced me to air conditioning.

I snatched two of the biscuits left over from breakfast the next morning and hid them in the bag of butter beans along with a handful of dried hot peppers. I knew Jake would be hungry and his canned stuff wasn't good for breakfast. I wanted to take him a jar of jam, but I couldn't figure out a way to get it out of the house. Maybe tomorrow.

He had already exited the cotton house and was sitting on the ground at our spot in the woods when I got there. He was whittling on a forked hickory stick.

"Morning, Mister Ted."

"Hey, Jake. What're you making?"

"Making you a slingshot. In fact, I gon' make us both one. A good slingshot can be a mighty formidable weapon. I used to be able to knock down a rabbit wid one. You knows, in de Bible, little David killed a giant wid one."

"Yeah, that was Goliath."

"Dat's right."

"I brought you a couple of biscuits. I wanted to bring you some jam. I will tomorrow."

"I gots dis can of sausages I'll eat wid dem. What else you gots in dat bag?"

"Some butter beans my mother is selling to Mrs. Blossom."

"Butter beans be one of my favorites, cooked wid a piece of smoked hog jowl, but widout no fire I couldn't cook 'em anyways."

While Jake washed down his biscuits and sausage with a fruit jar of branch water, I picked up the stock of the slingshot he was making. I held the stem in my left hand, stretched out my arm and sighted down between the fork. Near the tops of the two stems of the fork he had carved a trench completely around each. I asked, "What're these for?"

"Dat's so when I ties de rubber strip down it will stay. I gots a piece of an old tire tube I'll make dem out of. De only thing I don't have is something to make de pouch, you knows, de part dat holds de rock."

"What do you need?"

"The tongue from an old shoe would make two of 'em."

"I'll see what I can do."

"De mail rider come early dis morning. I peeked through a crack in de cotton house and seed him. De letter be gone. I sho hopes dem whiskey police shows up. Otherwise, I gon' be eating nail soup."

Mrs. Blossom wasn't too sociable. She came to the screen

door, took the bag, gave me a quarter, and said, "Tell your momma I said thanks."

I supposed she was feeling bad that my daddy wouldn't have a job before long, so not wanting to prolong her misery, I said, "Thank you very much, Mrs. Blossom." Then I started walking off the porch.

I was startled when she came out onto the porch and called out, "You come back here, sugar boy." I thought that nickname was known only to my family, but I guessed she could have heard it somewhere.

She walked across the porch, dropped to one knee, and hugged me real tight. She smelled like fried chicken. Then she released me, stood up, stuffed a paper dollar into my pants pocket, turned and disappeared into the house. She was dabbing at her face with her apron.

The next thing I saw was Mr. Blossom sitting on the front steps of Miss Lena's store, removing his muddy brogans. He left them sitting there beside the steps before entering the store in his socks. I looked all about, saw no one anywhere, quickly took advantage of the opportunity, then hit the woods running.

I was in my element—the woods. Circling around the sawmill, I took the short cut which took me directly to the Mill Creek. I found the broken limb on the big sweet gum tree and splashed into the creek heading toward the still. When I got to the spot which led toward Poudlum's house, I hesitated a moment, wanting to take him with me, but I figured he was probably picking cotton—what was left of it, that is.

Soon I crawled into mine and Poudlum's original hiding place, parted the leaves, and peered across the Saltifa. Everything was quiet, with just the sound of the running water, the birds, and the squirrels. However, something had been going on because there was a big mound covered by a heavy canvas tarp. I was just about to gather up enough courage to go up the bank and cross over on the fallen tree when I heard a sound that didn't belong. At first it sounded like a giant house fly in the distance. It was coming from down the creek. I cocked my ear and strained to listen as the sound became louder, then I recognized it—someone was coming up the creek in a motor boat!

My first inclination was to run, but instead I nestled deeper into the leaves, gripped my stick tighter, and reminded myself that I was here to find out who actually made the whiskey.

When the boat came into view I saw that it was a big one, about twice the size of the one I had hidden up the creek, and it was loaded with boxes and sacks. The driver was seated in the back guiding it with the handle on the motor. He was wearing overalls and a blue work shirt, with a slouchy felt hat partially covering his darkly bearded face. I had never seen him before.

The motor went dead and the boat's forward motion caused the front end to slide into the bank across the creek from me. The whiskey maker climbed over his supplies, grabbed a rope, stepped out on the bank, pulled the boat aground, then tied the rope to a small tree.

The next thing he did scared me and caused me to realize the graveness of my situation. He went back to the boat, pulled out a long double-barreled shotgun, walked up to the money tree and leaned it against the tree.

The mound under the tarp turned out to be firewood. I knew it was dry, because after he started his fire, the smoke was white rather than dark. As it spread out and drifted up into the canopy of the forest, it was almost invisible.

After the whiskey maker started cooking he began to unload his boat. I counted six of the big boxes. I knew each contained forty-eight empty pint bottles. It looked like it was going to be a big week.

It wasn't long before I began to regret having come there. I had a cramp in one of my legs, black ants were biting me and I had too many itches to count, but I knew I had to suffer and be real careful because if I was discovered, then my whole plan would be ruined, not to mention that the whiskey maker would probably shoot me with his shotgun, throw me in the creek, and I would float down to the Tombigbee where the turtles would eat me.

With these and other horrible thoughts going through my mind, I began inching backwards every time his back was toward me. As he went about his evil task, I kept inching and inching until I felt the cool water of the Mill Creek on my feet. Only then did I rise into a crouch and began walking softly back up the creek. When I was certain that I was beyond his hearing, I took a deep breath and began running.

I DIDN'T GO back the way I had come because I needed to talk to Poudlum. I walked past the burnt-out cotton house and made my way through the field full of black stubs which used to be cotton plants. I figured I would find them on the back side of the house picking cotton, but then I saw Poudlum coming down the front porch steps with his arm wrapped around an empty gallon milk jug.

Buster saw me before Poudlum did and he came out from underneath the porch with a low growl in his throat. Then he stopped short. Recognizing me and seeing my new stick, he sat down on the ground and started thumping it with his tail. "Hey, Poudlum," I called out.

"Ted!" he said with a big toothy smile. "What you doing over dis way?"

"Looking for you. I thought you'd be picking cotton."

"I wuz. Ain't much left. Dey don't need me."

"You on you way to get some milk?"

"Naw, just taking Miss Annie Pearl's jug back. My moma sez we can't 'ford no more milk, what wid de cotton burning up."

I noticed his smile had disappeared. "You mind if I walk along with you?"

"Shoot no. Be a pleasure to have you wid me."

I asked, "How's your momma and daddy?"

"Dey ain't too good 'cause ain't gon' be nuff cotton money to pay de taxes. Don't know what we gon' do."

"Why don't your momma and daddy sell some timber to raise some money?"

"Dey always said dey saving it fo' our education, but den dey decided dey gon' hafta sell it."

"Well?"

"You knows who buys and sells all de timber around here."

"Old Man Cliff Creel!"

"Uh huh, dat's right, and he won't give us nothin fo' it."

"Then find someone else who'll buy it."

"My daddy tried dat too, but won't nobody talk to him 'bout it. He say he figures dat old man done got to everybody."

Everyday, that old man grew more despicable, and so did my resolve to see that he got paid in kind. "Poudlum, is y'alls cow black and white spotted and wearing a cow bell?"

"Yeah, dat's Old Sukie. Sho does miss her."

"Well, you won't be missing her long, 'cause we're gonna get her back."

"Who is?"

"Me and you."

"How we gon' do dat."

"I'm not sure yet."

Miss Annie Pearl was out back inside her chicken pen with a pail of corn she was scattering on the ground for the birds pecking away around her feet. I called out to her. "Hey, Miss Annie Pearl, me and Poudlum brought your milk jug back."

She shooed the chickens away from her feet, looked up and said, "Howdy, boys. Just set it there on the edge of the porch. Y'all be needing some more milk?"

Before Poudlum could say anything I answered, "Yes, ma'am, we need a gallon of sweet milk, a gallon of buttermilk, and two pounds of butter."

"Y'all go down to the spring house and fetch it up to the porch. I'll be there directly."

When we got back she was transferring eggs from her doubled up apron into a basket. When we placed the milk and butter on the porch she asked, "Want me to put it on the Robinsons' account?"

"No, ma'am, we gonna pay cash," I said as I handed her the dollar bill Mrs. Blossom had given me. I was thankful she didn't ask any questions, just gave me my change, put the butter in a bag and said, "Now, you boys skedaddle before that butter melts."

Poudlum had questions though. We were barely out of the yard when he asked, "Where you get dat paper dollar?"

"Miss Blossom gave it to me this morning."

"Why she do dat?"

"I don't know. Well, I sorta know, but I don't know how to explain it."

"Why you spend part of it on milk for us?"

There he goes again, I thought, but I decided to tell him one more time. "Because y'all ain't got no milk."

We walked for a good ways in silence, then Poudlum said, "Well, we's mighty grateful, and I gon' find some way to pay you back."

By the time we got back to the Robinsons' house I had figured out when and how to get their cow back. It would have to be Sunday morning while everyone was at church, but I would need some help. I gratefully placed the heavy milk jug on their porch, rubbed my arching arm and said, " Poudlum, I know how you can pay me back."

"You does? Den just tell me."

"I need you to help me all day Sunday."

"Well, sho I will in de afternoon, but I gots to go to church in de mawning."

"I'm supposed to, too, but we got to find a way to get out of it. Pretend you're sick or something and meet me behind Miss Lena's store between ten and eleven o'clock in the morning. Can you do it?"

"Sho I can. Come Sunday mawning, I gon' have one powerful bellyache."

16

School Clothes

I was real hungry, but I didn't want to be seen around Miss Lena's store today, so before I got to it I cut through the woods behind the Hicks place and came out at my grandfather's house.

As usual at this time of day, Pa Will was sound asleep in his rocking chair on the front porch. Ma Tine had a brush broom and was sweeping the front yard. I had watched her make those brooms before. She would take a half dozen small saplings about five feet tall and tie them into a bundle with the brushy ends all together at one end to form a yard broom. Most everybody's yard was bare and sandy with no grass, and a brush broom was a good way to keep it clean. Her yard looked clean to me. I supposed she just liked to see the lines the brush broom made in the dirt. "Hey, Ma Tine, how y'all doing."

She looked up from her yard cleaning and said, "Why, sugar boy, where on earth did you come from? I didn't see you coming down the road."

"I came through the woods."

"You best stay out of them woods, specially this time of the year, because the snakes are real bad. I killed one early this morning, right here in the yard." She turned her head and spat a stream of snuff juice which left a long brown stain in her clean yard, then she turned back toward me and asked, "You hungry?"

"Yes, ma'am, I'm real hungry."

"That don't surprise me none. Come on in the kitchen."

No matter what time of day, there was always a plate of biscuits in her oven. She took one out and bored a hole down into it with her finger, then she filled the hole with cane syrup, handed it to me and said, "Sit down at the table and I'll pour you a glass of milk."

She stayed and talked until I finished so there was no way I could snatch an extra one. I knew Jake would like one so I just asked, "Could I have another one to eat while I walk?"

"Good Lord, child, you must have worms." She bored another hole in another biscuit and wrapped it in a piece of waxed paper. "There, now you won't have to worry about getting your hands sticky with syrup."

I FOUND JAKE right where I had left him, in the woods behind the cotton house. "Didn't 'spect you back so soon," he said, "'specially wid another biscuit."

"I got something else for you," I said, reaching into my pocket and pulling out the tongue from Mr. Blossom's shoe.

Jake laughed and laughed when I told him how I had cut it out while Mr. Blossom was in the store.

"You is mighty fast wid yo' pocket knife. Dat man gon' be wondering for years what in de world happened to his shoe tongue. But de important thing is dat now I can finish de slingshots. I already got de rubbers on 'em—all we needs is de pouch."

He went right to work. With his knife he trimmed the leather into two oval-shaped pieces, then drilled tiny holes on the edge of each one. Next, he took a piece of fine cord and attached the pouch to the end of the rubber strips.

"I be finished here in a minute. If you would go down to de branch and fetch us a few rocks, 'bout de size of a marble, den you can try it out."

When I got back with a pocket full of rocks, Jake handed me the finished slingshot and said, "Dis one is yours. Mine got longer rubber strips on it. Go ahead, try it out."

I thought it was beautiful.

Jake watched me place a rock in the pouch. Then he demonstrated as he said, "Now, grip the stock tight, straighten yo' left arm out and lock yo' elbow. Hold de pouch 'tween yo' thumb and forefinger, pull it all de way back to yo' right eye, close yo' left eye, pick out a target, sight 'tween de fork and let it fly."

I followed his instructions, picked out a poplar tree about twenty yards away, and released the pouch. Zing! Whack!

"Hey, dat's real good fo' yo' first shot!"

I was stunned at the velocity of the rock when it struck the tree. "Good Lord, Jake, you could knock out something bigger then a rabbit with this thing."

"I 'spect so, and you can improve yo' accuracy if you uses a marble."

"Huh?"

"Dat's 'cause a marble be perfectly round. Hard to find a perfect rock. "Try another shot."

I shot three more rocks, picking a smaller tree each time, and didn't miss until the last one.

"Dat's good shooting. If you practice a lot, den you gon' get real good."

"You gonna try yours out?" I asked.

"Not right now. I gon' have plenty of time for dat later, after you be gone. Nothing to do but sit around in dese woods. Can't stand to stay in dat cotton house no mo, 'cept at night to sleep. Done read yo' last *Grit* paper fo' or five times; fact I just 'bout got it memorized." He let out a long sigh, then continued, "And today just be Wednesday. Don't know if I can stand three mo nights in dat cotton house. I sho would like to light out tonight."

"You can't do that, Jake, they'll catch you for sure; besides you only have to stay in the cotton house for two more nights."

"Uh, you said you knows a way I can slip outta here on Sunday while all de excitement of de bootlegger being caught be going on. Dat's three mo nights."

"That's right, but you got to move out of here late Saturday night and sleep in the woods behind the sawmill."

"Sleep over dere in de woods—how come?"

"Because you're gonna be moving by midafternoon Sunday and you can't very well cross the road in broad daylight."

"I wish you'd tell me de details of dis plan you gots."

"I will as we go along. By dark on Sunday night you'll be in Choctaw County, then if you travel all night along highway eighty-four you'll be in Waynesboro, Mississippi, by daylight Monday morning."

"How you knows all dis?"

"Uncle Curvin told me. Once you're in Waynesboro, then you can buy yourself a bus ticket all the way to California."

"How I gon' do dat wid only twelve dollars and thurty cents?"

"You said you was gonna trust me."

Jake pulled out his big red handkerchief, mopped his face, got a faraway look on his face like he was million miles away and said, "I did, and I will. Any particular place I ought to sleep in dem woods behind the sawmill?"

"Just far enough into them so nobody can see you, but come Sunday morning, walk straight south until you come to the Mill Creek. When you reach it, you may have to go up or down it a little ways, but sooner or later you'll find a big sweet gum tree with a broken limb. Me and Poudlum will meet you there around one o'clock."

"Poudlum? Why he gon' be wid you?"

"'Cause me and him gonna take their milk cow back from Old Man Creel's house while everybody's in church."

His eyes grew wide. "Lawd have mercy, child! Y'all ain't gon' do no such thing."

"Yeah we are. I got it all figured out. I remember a gate being down that fence line from where that mean dog tried to eat me. I mean to take old Sukie out that gate, then we'll stay in the woods all the way to Poudlum's house, except when we have to cross the road."

"What y'all gon' do 'bout dat big red dog?"

"He likes to eat raw chicken. I'm gonna take him a live one, throw it over the fence and while he's having Sunday dinner we'll get the cow out the gate."

"Dat sounds good, but I be worried about you little fellas."

It was beginning to get hot even in our shady spot in the woods. With the heat came the midday quiet when even the woods creatures were taking a nap. I knew it was time for me to be getting home.

I wrapped the rubber straps around the stock of my slingshot and put it in my back pocket. My stick was leaning against a tree. I picked it up, told Jake I would bring him something to eat tomorrow, and thanked him for the slingshot.

"Dat slingshot be like a spark compared to de sun if you manages to help me be a free man."

I was thinking about what he had just said when he interrupted my thoughts. "How far back does dese woods behind dis cotton house go?"

"Goes on forever far as I know. I've been most a mile up that branch."

"I think I gon' try to scare me up a rabbit dis afternoon, den if I go far enough back in de woods I can build myself a fire and roast him. I needs me a hot meal. Sho would like to have myself a mess of greens and a pork chop, but a rabbit will be good."

"I guess that'll be all right."

"Dat'll take care of dis day, but I don't know what I'll do to kill de time fo' three mo days."

"Why don't you write some songs?"

"Do what?"

"Yeah, why don't you write some of them blues songs about sleeping in a cotton house or in the woods? You got a pencil and paper."

"Lawdy me, now here you is telling me how to write de blues, but you knows, dat's a real good idea."

THERE WAS ANOTHER big storm late that night, and this one brought hail. The heavy rain had already roused me from a deep sleep, then the intensification of noise from the hail transported me to full awareness. At first it sounded like the time I had taken a shotgun shell apart to see what was inside of it and poured the metal pellets into a tin plate. Then the hail got bigger and thicker and it turned into a huge roar. It ended as suddenly as it started. After a while the only sound was the steady dripping of the water sliding off the tin roof into the rain barrel. I thought Jake was probably glad to be inside that cotton house tonight.

Then I slept and when I awoke I knew it wasn't early anymore because slivers of light from the morning sun were flowing through the crack in the bedroom door. I watched the tiny particles of dust floating in the air and marveled at how they were completely invisible outside the rays of light. I looked around and saw that the room was empty. I rolled out of bed, grabbed my pants and saw that my back pocket was also empty. My slingshot was gone. I had to find Fred.

While I was washing my face and hands on the porch I spotted him just past the wood pile and the sounds I heard told me that he had my slingshot.

I stood behind him, knowing that he hadn't heard me walk up, and saw that he wasn't doing too well at it. His target was an empty motor oil can which he had stuck up on top of a ancient cedar fence post where the fence itself had long ago rotted away.

After watching his fourth miss I said, "Let me show you how to do that."

He jumped pretty good and said, "Why the heck you want to sneak up on somebody like that for?'

"You got any more rocks?"

"There's a pile right there," he said, pointing toward his feet. "Can't hit nothing with this thing anyway."

I took the slingshot from his outstretched hand, selected a stone, loaded it, drew back, took careful aim and released. Zing! Ding! The can toppled to the ground.

"How the heck did you do that?"

"Go put the can back up and I'll show you."

When he returned I handed the weapon back to him and said, "Here, try another shot, but listen real careful while I talk you through it."

I gave him instructions exactly as Jake had given them to me and when he hit the can he said, "This thing is great."

Then he asked a question which I was totally unprepared for. "Where did you get this thing?"

When I hesitated he asked again, "Well, where?"

I figured I had to think of a believable lie fast, but then I thought that I didn't really have to lie. I could say where I got it, just not when. "Jake make it for me."

"That nigger from the sawmill, the one that's an escaped convict?"

"Yeah, the same colored man who made my stick."

"When did he give you that slingshot?"

This was going to be close to a lie, but not quite. "A while back."

"Where you been keeping it?"

"I had hid it under the house."

Now that was a lie. "Where is mother and Ned?" I asked quickly.

"They gone with Uncle Curtis to pick butter beans. Let's go see what they left on the stove, then we'll shoot this thing some more."

While we were having biscuits and jam Fred began to study the slingshot, turning it over in his hand, examining every part of it. After a while he said, "I believe I can make one of these."

I seized the opportunity. "Sure you can. All you need to do is cut a forked oak or hickory stick out of the woods, find an old tire tube, a piece of leather and some twine, then just put it all together."

A few minutes later I watched while he disappeared into the woods with our father's hand saw. Then I disappeared in the opposite direction with two biscuits, a pint of blackberry jam, and a quart of last year's peaches. Jake ate half the jar of peaches before he put the cap back on and said he would save the rest for supper."

"Did you get a rabbit yesterday?"

"Sho did. Roasted him and ate de whole thing. It was

mighty good, but not nearly so good as yo' momma's peaches."

I noticed several pieces of paper sticking out of the pocket of his bib overalls. "You been writing some." I asked.

"Sho has, been writing like crazy. Done got inspired being out in dese woods so long. When I gets to California I gon' sing some blues like dey never heard."

THE ANNUAL RITUAL of ordering school and winter clothes took place at our house that night. My brothers were finished and it was my turn. My mother turned the wick of the kerosene lamp up because the light of day was just about faded away. "Step on up here closer to me," She said.

She had a tape measure which she used to measure my arms, my waist, my neck, my legs, everything except my feet. For them she had me stand on a piece of paper while she knelt on the floor and used a pencil to trace the outline of my foot. She cut that outline out with scissors and would later mail it in to Sears and Roebuck for a pair of shoes along with an order for two new pair of jeans and two new shirts. These along with the hand-me-downs from Fred would be my wardrobe until next year. When she was finished she moved the lamp, all her measurements, the paper footprints, and the order forms to the kitchen table to complete her motherly task.

I heard her in there talking. At first I thought she was talking to herself, then I realized she was praying. "Lord, we got to have these clothes for these young 'uns. I don't know how we're going to pay for them, what with J. D. soon to be out of work. I been saving my vegetable and egg money, but it won't be nearly enough. If by some miracle you could see your way clear to help us out, well, then we would surely be appreciative. Amen."

I wanted to rush in there and tell her that a miracle was on the way, but I knew I couldn't risk disappointing her. I had to make sure that miracle happened first. Just three more days.

17

Lying On Sunday

Time drug by like pouring syrup on a cold morning. I didn't think Friday would ever end. After an early morning visit with Jake we decided that would be the last time we would meet until Sunday afternoon. "No need to take chances," he had said.

Night came, but there was no relief from the heat. Fred performed his feat of air conditioning which let me finally slip into a dream-filled world of being chased across creeks and through woods by bootleggers and big red bulldogs.

I awoke with a start, was relieved to be safe in my own bed, and happy that it was Saturday because I would have my paper route to pass the day.

From a distance I saw the mail rider stuffing my papers into the box. The dust had settled by the time I pulled them out and placed them into my bag. A few minutes later I was on Mrs. Blossom's front porch knocking on the wooden edge of her screen door saying, "Mrs. Blossom, I got—"

Suddenly the door opened and there stood Mr. Blossom

with his great protruding belly. "Mrs. Blossom ain't here, son. She's done gone on to Mobile to look for us a place to stay. She won't be back."

I didn't know what to say. When I regained my composure I said, "I'm sorry to hear that, sir. Uh, would you like a *Grit* paper?"

"Naw, I got no time to read. I got to get on down to the sawmill."

I couldn't resist it. I looked down at his shoes and saw his sock where the tongue should have been on his left foot. Then I noticed him cock his head and start looking at me hard, so I immediately diverted my eyes and began backing off the porch. My slingshot was in my back pocket with the rubber straps hanging loose. Although I felt he wouldn't recognize a piece of his shoe tongue attached to them, I still didn't want to afford him the opportunity.

"Well, uh, thank you, sir. Please tell Mrs. Blossom I said hey." I pushed my paper bag, which was hanging from my shoulder by the strap, back behind me so it would cover my slingshot, turned and walked away.

I walked east on Center Point Road. I had only gone a little ways when I heard a car coming from towards Coffeeville. I watched until it pulled in front of Miss Lena's. I got a real bad feeling when I saw Sheriff Crowe get out of the car. He put his hat on, stretched, scratched himself, then walked into the store.

Miss Lena had electricity which kept the drink box cool and the box for Popsicles and ice cream frozen. She also had an electric window fan in the window directly behind the counter where she always stationed herself. The windowsill was about six inches over my head. I could stand beneath it undetected and hear the conversation from within, despite the whine of the big saw blade at the mill. I heard the voice of the fat sheriff saying, "Been all over this damn county looking for that nigger and ain't nobody seen hide nor hair of him. Don't make no sense. Seems like somebody would have seen him or he would have left a trail somewhere. But it's my own damn fault—should've brought the bloodhounds with me when I come down here the first time."

I doubted they would have helped. Jake had had dogs on his trail before. He knew how to deal with them.

Miss Lena said, "Well, like I said, sheriff, ain't nobody round here seen him since the day before you came down here looking for him."

I could tell by the tone of her voice that she didn't like that sheriff any more than my Uncle Curvin did.

"How you know that, ma'am?"

"'Cause everybody comes in here and if they had, then somebody would've said something."

"That's what I figured—reason I stopped by here."

"Is there anything else I can do for you, sheriff."

My heart just about stopped when I heard his next question. "Let me ask you this, ma'am. Do you know of anybody around here that he hung around with, maybe spent time with?"

I knew Miss Lena had seen me come in and out of the store with Jake, but I wasn't sure if she knew I had spent a lot of time at the sawmill with him. I was relieved when I heard her answer, "No, nobody that I know of. You might want to talk to the men down at the sawmill."

"No. I done talked to all of them. You seen Curvin Murphy around anywhere?"

It was getting worse.

"I saw him go by early this morning. I believe he was going to help the Robinsons haul what's left of their cotton to the gin."

"I don't believe I know the Robinsons."

"They're the colored folks who—"

"Colored folks! You didn't tell me no niggers lived around here."

"I don't remember hearing you ask."

"Where they live?"

"You know where Old Man Cliff Creel lives?"

"Of course I know where Mr. Creel lives."

I was sure he did too. Probably stopped by there quite often to pick up some whiskey and some payoff money.

"After you pass his house you'll see a wagon path on your left. If you turn in there it will take you down to their place."

"You see or hear anything, ma'am, you get in touch with me. I'm gonna ride over to that nigger place and have me a look see. If they're harboring that convict I'm putting all of 'em in jail."

When I heard his heavy boots on the wooden floor, in a state of fright, I made a bad mistake. Instead of just going behind the store until he left, I started running. I was on the road before he came out of the store and saw me. I could feel his evil eyes boring into my back.

I heard the car door slam, the engine crank up, then the sound of the tires crunching on the gravel. Maybe he would turn his car around and just go on to where he had said he was going, but I doubted it. I figured it would look even worse if I stopped running, so I just kept going, forming lies in my head.

When he pulled up beside me, he hung his head out of the car window and said, "Hey, boy. Hold up here a minute."

I stopped and he ground the big car to a halt. There he was, right in front of me. "What you running from, boy?"

I was scared, but then I thought about what my father had told me about how I would encounter a lot of bullies during my life. I knew I couldn't use my stick, which I had a tight grip on, but I did know this man was a coward and a bully. No more than a cross between a snake and a mean dog in my mind. Maybe it was my guardian angel, which my mother had always assured me that I had, but for some reason a sense of clarity and confidence came over me.

I looked directly into his bloodshot eyes and said, "I ain't running from, I'm running to."

I could tell that wasn't the response he expected and it puzzled him for a moment, then he asked, "Well, what is it you're running to?"

I lifted my newspaper bag up in front of his eyes and said, "Running to deliver my papers 'cause I'm late."

He was a bully, but he wasn't stupid. I could tell he was searching for something while he looked at me. I think it was my cotton-top head that caused him to recognize me. "Wait a minute, didn't I see you at the cotton gin the other day with that gimpy Murphy runt?"

I knew the meaning of the word runt, and my uncle was a small man. But I didn't know the meaning of the other word, just that it was not complimentary, so I took exception to my uncle being called a bad name. "Yes sir, that was me, but my Uncle Curvin ain't gimpy."

"Course he is boy, and you gimpy in the head if you don't know it. You know anything about a nigger what's been working down at the sawmill?"

"No, sir."

"Yore Uncle Curvin say anything about him after y'all left the cotton gin?"

"No, sir."

"All right, you git on down the road with your papers, but I'm gonna be watching you. And you tell your uncle I'm looking for him."

"Yes, sir."

I didn't wait for him to turn his car around. I started walking and just listened to the sound of it. In a while I stopped, turned and looked down the road and watched him disappear over the hill.

I knew I had just told a passel of lies, but I figured the Lord would forgive me because I told them to such a bad person.

I wasn't worried about the Robinsons either because they didn't know anything about Jake's whereabouts. The sheriff would probably give them a difficult time, but that was about all he could do. Also, I knew Uncle Curvin could truthfully say he hadn't seen or talked to Jake, and if he had to lie about suggesting I contact him, then he would.

I looked over toward the cotton house and wondered if Jake had observed my encounter with the sheriff, hoping that if he had, that he wouldn't panic and start running. How funny, I thought, the person that fat sheriff was looking for had probably been looking right at him through a crack in the cotton house door.

I VISITED A while with everyone on my route because I wanted to make my job last the entire day; consequently it was well after the dinner hour when I finished the eastern half. Miss Lena's store came into view and my mouth watered when I thought about the things inside.

When I passed the Blossoms' house I noticed several boxes sitting on the porch. I supposed it wouldn't be long before Mr. Blossom would be gone, too. Now I knew why Mrs. Blossom had hugged me and given me a dollar bill when I brought her the butter beans. It was because she knew it would probably be the last time she would ever see me.

The sawmill workers had come and gone. The store was deserted except for Miss Lena. I went straight to the drink box, lifted the lid and pulled out a strawberry Nehi, then I took a dime box of saltine crackers off the shelf. At the counter, I watched while Miss Lena lifted the round wooden cover off the hoop of cheese and sliced me a piece.

"You can sit on the drink box and eat if you want to," She said.

She only let folks she liked sit on her drink box. I had seen her shoo people off of it before. I set my drink, crackers and cheese on it, then I hopped up beside them. The painted metal felt smooth and cool.

"That sorry excuse for a sheriff didn't scare you, did he?"

"No, ma'am."

"What did he have to say?"

I had a mouth full of cheese and crackers and I had to wash it down before I could answer. "He just asked me if I knew anything about Jake. And, oh yeah, he said he was looking for Uncle Curvin."

"He asked me about Curvin too. Why you think he's looking for Curvin?"

I told her about us having seen him at the cotton gin on Monday and about his conversation with Uncle Curvin. "I 'spect he just wants to ask Uncle Curvin if he warned Jake that he was coming down here looking for him."

"Curvin ain't got no reason to have done that."

"No, ma'am."

"You don't think the Robinsons are hiding him, do you?"

"No, ma'am, I know they ain't, 'cause I been over there."

"Well, I don't care if he was an escaped convict. He didn't bother nobody and he was real polite. I liked him, didn't you?"

"Yes, ma'am, I liked him a lot."

"I hope he got clean away, hope he's already over yonder in Mississippi somewhere."

He will be come Monday, I thought to myself.

My next stop was with Aunt Minnie, Aunt Sadie, and Uncle Bud, and yes, they were on the front porch dipping snuff, rocking and spitting. They found a nickel between the three of them and immediately split the paper in three parts. Aunt Minnie said, "They're some baked sweet potatoes and cornbread in the oven, sugar boy, if you're hungry."

"No, ma'am, thank you, I ate me something at Miss Lena's store."

"Well, then get you a drink of water and sit a spell with us. You heard anything about a nigger escaped convict being loose around here?"

Uncle Bud and Aunt Sadie were reading, but Aunt Minnie wanted to talk. "Yes, ma'am, but ain't no need for y'all to worry about that."

Aunt Minnie leaned over and spat a big mouth full of snuff juice and asked, "Well, how some you say that, sugar boy? We been scared to death around here."

"'Cause I know him. He worked over at the sawmill and he wouldn't hurt a fly, much less y'all, and he's gone now anyway." I knew the last part was a lie, but it wouldn't be one tomorrow.

That seems to satisfy her because she started reading her part of the paper. I got myself a drink of their good well water, said good bye and headed out to finish my work.

It was Sunday morning and I lay in bed listening to the activity of my family. I heard my father and Ned when they walked off the porch, heard them call Old Bill from under the house, then the rattle of the chain when they hooked it to his collar so he wouldn't follow them into the woods and scare away the wild turkeys.

Outside the window I could hear Fred getting out of the wash tub and I knew it wouldn't be long before my mother would be back to roust me out of bed. She had already been in once and she didn't like to have to come back. I practiced having a painful look on my face and waited. I didn't have to wait long.

"Am I gonna have to get a switch to get you out of the bed?" She said after she burst through the door.

"I got a bad bellyache, mother."

"You're gonna have a bad butt ache if you don't get out of that bed, wash your hands, and get to the breakfast table. And I mean right now."

She left the room before I could respond so I knew I had to get up and begin the second phase of my fake illness. I crept into the kitchen holding my stomach, pulled out a chair and sat down. I could see her watching me out of the corner of her eye.

Phase two was going to take a lot of will power, but I knew I was up to it. I had to be.

She had a plate in front of me with a biscuit split open and smothered with gravy, its steam rising toward my face. Next to that were thin slices of fried sweet potatoes. They were brown and crispy, just the way I liked them. I had to keep swallowing the saliva that welled up in my mouth, but I just sat there and stared at the food, never making a move to touch it.

"Don't just sit there, son, eat your breakfast."

"Can't. My belly hurts too bad."

I tried to make my breathing sound labored and finally she gave in. I was so thankful because phase three, if it had been needed, entailed eating some soap while I was bathing so I would throw up.

"All right, you can go on back to bed. If you get to feeling better, then walk on down to your Uncle Curtis's house.

We'll be having Sunday dinner there after church."

"Yes, ma'am, I will if I do."

A while later Fred poked his head in and said in a loud whisper, "I know you're faking. Next week will be my turn."

Then I heard Uncle Curtis's truck and knew it was my cousin Robert coming to pick us up. Fred closed the door.

As soon as the sound of the truck's engine faded away I was up and headed for the kitchen. I found my breakfast plate in the oven and in less than two minutes it was clean. It was a good breakfast. I hoped Poudlum and Jake had one, too, because we were going to need our strength today.

I selected three of my least-favorite marbles and put them into my pocket. Next I gathered my weapons, the stick and the slingshot, then I was on the move.

18

Up a Tree

I took the trail to Friendship Road, then hugged the edge of the woods the rest of the way, in case some late church-goers might come along. When I got to Center Point Road I stopped, looked up and down the road, and listened hard. The only sound was the raspy call of a crow high overhead. There was no motion anywhere. Everything was so still it could have been a painted picture.

I dashed across the road to the front door of the store, pressed my face to the glass, and looked at the clock behind the counter. It was straight up eleven o'clock. We had a little over an hour before people would be out of church and moving about. We had to move. I started toward the rear of the store, hoping to find Poudlum waiting there.

He wasn't, but before I had time to get alarmed, he emerged from the edge of the woods and called out, "Over here."

"What you doing in the woods?" I asked.

"Just didn't want to be hanging out behind dat sto' by myself."

"How come?"

"'Fraid somebody might see me and think I be up to some devilment."

"We are. We up to a lot of devilment, but there's no one around to see us 'cause everybody is at church. Let's get going. First we're gonna go through the woods to my Uncle Bud's house and steal a chicken."

"A chicken? I thought we gon' steal a cow."

"We are, but first we got to steal a chicken."

"How come?"

"'Cause we need to feed one to that big mean dog. While he's having Sunday dinner we'll make off with your cow."

As we walked through the woods I asked Poudlum if they had a visit from the sheriff yesterday.

"Sho did. How you know 'bout dat?"

"Heard him tell Miss Lena he was coming to y'all's place looking for Jake. What did he say to y'all?"

"'Bout scared us all to death. Went all through de house like he be looking fo' something, yelling about how he gon' put us all in de jail house 'cause we be hiding Jake. We don't know what he be talking 'bout."

"I know it. Sorry y'all had to put up with that. That old sheriff, he's just a bully, so tell your momma and them not to worry about it. He can't do nothing to y'all."

"I wonder why he thinks we be hiding Jake?"

"Probably 'cause y'all the only colored folks that live here bouts."

EVERYBODY CROPPED THE wings of their chickens so they couldn't fly out of their pens. This was done by cutting the feathers off the ends of their wings with a pair of scissors leaving a straight line of short stubby nubs where the long tapered ones had been. They could still flap, squawk, and run, but they couldn't fly. The pens were constructed out of chicken wire, which was much finer than fence wire. The holes were too small for the chickens to get out or for foxes and other varmints to get in.

The old rusted hinges on the gate to Uncle Bud's chicken pen groaned when I opened it. The chickens started cackling and retreated to the far side of the pen as if they knew we were up to no good.

"What if somebody in de house hears all dis fuss and comes out here?"

"Ain't nobody in the house, they gone to church."

"What if one of 'em didn't go?"

"If one of 'em didn't go, then they won't be able to hear us anyway because they'd be dead. Speaking of church, how'd you get out of going this morning?"

"Faked a bellyache. Thought I wuz gon' get a whupping from Momma, fo' she finally let me go back to bed. 'Spect I probably will get one fo' de day be over."

"I doubt it. If everything works out, then you gonna be a hero when you get home about midafternoon."

"Midafternoon! I gots to be home fo' everybody gets back from church."

"Poudlum, after we get your cow home we got to make one more trip to that whiskey still."

"Uh-uh!"

I knew the time had come when I needed to tell him everything. I started out by telling him where Jake had been all week, where he was going to meet us, and what we were going to do. I went on to tell him how Jake and I had written a letter to the whiskey police and how we expected them to haul Old Man Creel away when he came home later today with his load of moonshine. His eyes grew wider and wider as I talked, but when I finished he was nodding in agreement.

"So when dat old man gets home he gon' have mo to worry 'bout dan our cow."

"If the Lord's willing and them mail riders did their job, he will. We ain't never gonna tell nobody about none of this. As far as we know that cow just got loose and wandered on back home. Now, let's quit standing around here in this chicken pen and catch one. Watch where you step." I added that last part because I purely hated the feel of chicken do squeezing up between my bare toes and I figured Poudlum felt the same way.

Them chickens made a real ruckus when we went after them, flapping their useless wings and running in all directions. We finally cornered a young pullet. I fastened the gate while Poudlum tucked the bird under his arm.

On the way out of the yard I spotted a piece of rope on the back porch. "Will that cow come to you if you call her?"

"I doubt it. She gives good milk, but she be dumb."

I grabbed the rope and said, "Come on, let's get moving."

The chicken got quiet and we made good time through the woods, coming out about fifty yards from the old man's house. After looking and listening, we dashed across the road into the woods on the other side and stopped at the big loblolly pine tree I had spied from.

I went over the plan with Poudlum, then I gave him the rope. I took the chicken and we walked to the edge of the woods where we immediately heard the tinkle of old Sukie's bell. There she was, a good thirty yards inside the gate.

Looking to my left toward the house, as expected, I saw that Old Man Creel's car was gone, but I didn't see the dog anywhere.

"I don't see that dog, Poudlum."

"Maybe he be sleeping somewhere. Let's just go get de cow, keep dis chicken and eat it ourselves."

"No, can't take that chance. Go on up to the gate and wait for me. I'm gonna walk down the fence toward the house. The closer down there we can keep him the better."

I was much closer to the house than I wanted to be when the dog saw me before I saw him. I heard a rumbling growl and then I saw him coming out from underneath the table where the old man and the preacher had sat and drunk their whiskey.

Before he could charge I threw the luckless pullet over the fence as hard as I could.

At first he was torn between coming after me or going for the chicken. I knew this because of the way his head turned from me to the chicken, back to me, then unable to resist, he went for the bird which was running and flapping for its life. A short burst and he caught it and crushed it with his massive jaws.

I turned and started running down the fence line yelling, "Open the gate, Poudlum."

When I got there he had slid the latch back, but was

struggling, unable to open it by himself. It was a big gate, wide enough to drive a truck through when completely opened, but the hinges were worn out and the bottom was dragging on the ground.

We each knew what to do. Without talking we got our hands underneath one of the boards near the bottom, lifted and pulled until we had it open far enough to get the cow through it. We stuck our heads through the opening, looking toward the house. The dog was on his stomach with the chicken between his front paws, ripping away at it. The only thing I didn't like about it was that his head was pointed toward us and he would be able to watch us, but it was now or never, so I said, "Come on, let's get the rope around the cow's neck and get out of here. Don't run, just walk real easy like."

While we walked to where the cow stood, I kept my eye on the dog. He continued with his Sunday dinner, but every few moments he would stop, raise his head, and look directly at us.

When we reached the cow I said, "Put the rope on her, she knows you."

While Poudlum got the rope tied I never took my eyes off the dog. I knew he could hurt us bad, maybe even kill us.

We both started pulling while Poudlum talked softly to the cow. "Come on Old Sukie. We's gon' take you home where you belongs."

I was greatly relieved when she lifted her head and began following the lead of the rope, but then the cow bell around her neck began to jingle loudly.

The dog's head came up from the chicken again and

this time it didn't go back down. I knew then that I should have taken my pocket knife and cut the bell off her before we had started moving her.

We were almost to the gate when the bulldog lost interest in the chicken.

"Pull harder," I told Poudlum. "We got to get through that gate and close it."

I moved behind the cow and started pushing on her rump while Poudlum pulled hard on the rope. Just as Old Sukie was halfway through the gate the dog stepped over and away from the mangled pile of feathers and began to growl.

When we were through the gate I knew we didn't have much time. In fact, I suspected we were out of time.

"Quick, Poudlum. Help me close the gate."

As soon as we got our hands on the heavy gate I knew it was too late. I heard the rhythm of his big heavy paws beating the ground on a dead run and I knew we would never get the gate closed before he got there.

I grabbed Poudlum's arm and yelled, "Run! Run hard as you can!" We were half way across the strip of tall grass when I glanced over my shoulder and saw the bulldog tearing through the open gate.

I yelled, "The big pine tree where we stopped! Hit it on the run and start climbing!"

Poudlum was three steps ahead of me when I thought about dropping my stick to gain some speed, but I decided against it. If the dog caught us I could use it on him so that at least Poudlum could get away.

When we reached the edge of the woods I took one more

quick glance over my shoulder. He was gaining on us, but I figured we had a good chance if we made no mistakes. One stumble or slip and I knew we wouldn't make it.

Poudlum leapt for a low limb, grabbed it and was pulling himself up an instant before I did the same. I could feel the dog's hot breath on my heels as I grabbed for the second limb, then I was up next to Poudlum where both of us were hugging the tree trunk and breathing hard. The dog was snarling, growling, and scratching at the tree. He was reared up on the trunk and I could see tiny white feathers stuck in his face. We remained frozen to the tree until the dog finally backed off, sat on his haunches and stared at us.

"How long do you think before he'll leave?" I asked.

"Dat's a bull dog. I heard tell dey won't quit till dey dies."

"Does that mean we hafta stay up in this tree till he dies."

"Guess so, unless you can figure out a way to kill him."

"How am I supposed to kill that dog?"

"You could pretend like you wuz climbing down, den when he rushes at you, bash him in de head wid yo' stick."

I looked up through the limbs of the tree at the sun, concluded it was about half past eleven, and knew we had to do something soon. I also knew that if we had to just sit up in this tree until someone rescued us, then we would both probably be marched home and beaten severely with switches. On top of that we would miss the opportunities of robbing the bootleggers and getting Jake safely out of the county. We had to do something.

"All right," I said. "I'll give it a try. You hold on to my belt."

I hated the idea of getting that close to him, but relished the thought of rapping him on the head with my hickory stick. I twisted around so that instead of sitting on the limb I was laying across it on my belly. The dog got to his feet. I got a good grip on my stick with the leather strap around my wrist, then I lowered one foot to the limb below me while I told Poudlum, "Hang on to me real tight."

When my foot touched the lower limb he charged, reared up on the tree trunk, growling and snapping his powerful jaws. I quickly jerked my foot up, swung the stick with all my might and felt the jar of it all up my arm when it hit him on the right side of his head. It never fazed him. As soon as it bounced off his head, before I could lift it back up, he turned his head and grasped it tightly in his jaws. I knew immediately that he wasn't going to let it go. Then I lost my grip on the stick and the leather strap was pulled tight around my wrist when he dropped his front feet back to the ground. He started to back up and the leather cut deep into my skin while my belt was cutting into my belly. I gave up and slipped my hand out of the loop.

After I gained my former position, Poudlum and I watched while he viciously shook his massive head from side to side with my prized stick in his mouth.

"If 'en dat was yo' arm, den he would've done bit it off."

"I'm getting scared, Poudlum."

"Gittin' scared—I been scared ever since you first thought of dis whole thing."

"You got any other ideas?"

"Yo' slingshot might help, but we ain't go no rocks."

"I got three marbles."

"Dey probably be better dan rocks. How good is you wid it?"

"Not as good as Jake, but pretty good."

"If'en you could hit him in a vulnerable spot—like pop him in one of his eyes, den he might go away."

I pulled my slingshot out of my back pocket, dug out my three marbles, put two in my mouth and loaded the other one in the pouch.

The dog settled down on the ground where he was chewing on my stick, but he had his right side toward us, angling away so I couldn't get a bead on his eyes.

I waited a few moments hoping he would shift his position, but he just kept eating my stick.

"We gots to get out of here," Poudlum said. "Shoot him in de ear."

I aimed carefully, but just as I released he turned his head slightly and the marble struck him on the neck. I knew it stung him good because he leapt to his feet and began going in circles biting at the air as if he thought he had been stung by a wasp.

"Dat was almost a good shot. Let'm settle down fo' you shoots again."

He was back chewing on my stick in a few moments and this time he was facing us.

"Now you can go for dat eyeball," Poudlum said. Once again, I loaded up and took aim, but he just wouldn't keep his head still and my second marble landed right between his eyes and bounced off. The shot didn't bother him as much as the first one had.

"Dat dog has got one hard head. And we is running out of time," Poudlum moaned.

And I was down to my last marble.

19

Robin Hood

Turned out that I didn't need that last marble. While I was loading it into the pouch, in anticipation of my next shot, I heard a loud crash from toward the edge of the woods in the direction from which we had come.

Poudlum looked at me with big wide eyes and asked, "What you think dat wuz?"

I looked down to see that the dog had turned to face whatever had caused the noise. I could see his broad red back and his thick bobtail sticking straight up. Right below it hung his privates, like two big black walnuts in a tight leather sack.

That's when I heard the first sound, which was followed almost immediately by the second. Zing! Splat!

It was a sharp and biting sound when the rock hit the dog's sack. He went down like a fallen oak tree, pitching forward on his belly. I knew at once what had happened.

Poudlum didn't. "What happened? You didn't even shoot yo' marble."

"It's Jake," I answered.

The dog was over the initial shock, but not the pain. He was slowly crawling forward on his belly, then he looked over his shoulder, rolled his eyes up toward us and began to howl, low and mournfully. I almost felt sorry for him.

"Right in de nuts!" Poudlum said excitedly. "Dat dog's as good as dead. I knows I would be. Come on, let's get down."

Jake's deep voice came floating softly through the foliage.

"Y'all just stay where you is for a minute, till he crawls on off a ways."

I looked back toward the dog and saw that he was still belly crawling. Then he stopped, rolled to his side and licked himself, followed by another howl and some whimpering sounds. Finally he slowly struggled to his feet and started walking gingerly away.

Jake came out of the woods, stood underneath the tree, picked up my stick. He chuckled. "He sho is walking funny, ain't he."

"Jake! Boy, we are glad to see you."

"'Spect it be all right for y'all to come down now. Had a feeling y'all might get yo' selves into a tight spot and need some help, so I snuck over here to check on y'all. Figured out what was happening when I heard dat dog, snuck up and threw a limb over yonder to get him to turn around so I could get a good shot at him.

"Jake, what time do you think it is?"

"Nigh on to twelve o'clock. We needs to get back across de road fo' folks start coming home from church."

"Yeah, we need to move. Let's see where the cow went."

We peeked out of the edge of the woods just in time to see the dog go back through the gate considerably slower than he had come through it. Old Sukie had wandered about halfway across the strip of tall grass, grazing, with our rope dragging along beside her. Poudlum and I dashed out and retrieved the end of it while Jake stood guard. She followed willingly and we were ready to cross Center Point Road when I heard a vehicle coming from towards the church. We quickly pulled the cow back into the cover of the woods, where we watched and listened. When the car went by I saw that it was Mrs. Annie Pearl in her old Plymouth.

I knew something was wrong and I told Jake, "It's too early for her to be going home from church."

"I could be wrong about de time."

I shaded my eyes with my hand, took a quick glance at the sun. "No, I figure it's right at twelve o'clock, maybe a little before."

"Maybe de preacher let out early."

"No, he never does unless there's dinner-on-the-grounds, and that wasn't happening today. He always makes everybody sweat until ten or fifteen minutes after twelve, then everybody stands around and talks for another fifteen or twenty minutes. Something has got to be wrong."

We attempted the crossing again, saw no movement nor heard any sound, went across as fast as we could with the cow in tow.

We all breathed a sigh of relief once we were across and back under cover of the woods. We kept moving and it wasn't long before we came out behind the Robinsons' burnt-out cotton house.

"You think your folks are back from church yet." I asked Poudlum.

"Naw, dey won't be back until after two o'clock."

"How come so late?"

"You thinks yo' preacher keeps folks in church a long time—well, de one in our church carries on till after one o'clock."

"What time does he start preaching?"

"'Bout eleven o'clock, den he goes on and on, yelling and screaming wid amens and hallelujahs from all directions."

"How do you stand it?"

"I dozes a lot."

I had to tell Fred about this. There might be a market for his time-killing church games with the colored kids.

"Poudlum," Jake said, "since ain't nobody home, why don't you take de cow up to de house and tie her in de back? Be a nice surprise fo' yo' momma when she gets back. Me and Mister Ted gon' wait here fo' you."

Jake and I slid down into seating positions on the pine needles with our backs leaning against tree trunks. I looked across at him and realized that this would be the last day I would ever see him, and also the last time we would be alone. I felt sad and wished he could stay, tell me more stories, sing more blues songs, teach me more of the lessons of life and make me more toys. At the same time, I was glad he was going to get out of Clarke County and be free. I couldn't stand the thought of him being caught by Sheriff Crowe and being sent back to that prison in Georgia where he would have nothing to eat except corn pone and dry white beans.

"Jake?"

"Uh huh?"

"When you were in that prison, was there some bad people in there with you, or was they all like you?"

"Oh, no, dey was some awful bad folks in dere. Most of 'em deserved to be in dat place. Even mo' reason why I wanted to escape, 'cause I couldn't abide being around 'em."

"Well, you got away from all that and in a little while you're gonna be away from here and on your way to California."

"Does you think de time has come when you can tell me how I gon' be able to do dat?"

I knew it was time, so I told him where the whiskey still was, about the stray boat I had stashed just up the creek from it, about the money tree and how we were going to rob it to finance his trip, pay the Robinsons' delinquent property taxes, and solve my mother's money problems. Jake's reaction startled me because I didn't know what he was talking about when he said, "Lawd have mercy, you is a modern-day Robin Hood."

"Robin who?"

"Hood."

"Who is Robin Hood?"

"He wuz an outlaw in old England who robbed de rich people and gave to de po folks. I read about him while I was in prison."

I was thrilled to hear that I was being compared to someone in a book, so I said, "That's what I'll do when I grow up—rob rich people and bootleggers, then give it to poor folks."

"Naw, yo' don't wants to do dat. Dat Robin Hood story is more like a fairy tale. His intentions wuz noble, but robbing is still against de law. We'll do dis one today, but you gots to promise me you won't ever steal nothin' ever again in yo' life. Remember, when I played Robin Hood it landed me in de jail house."

I knew in my heart that Jake's advice was as good as gold, but I had another idea. "Okay, I promise you that Jake, but now I know what I'll really do when I grow up."

"What's dat?"

"I'm gonna figure out a way so that all the poor folks can become rich."

"Now, dat's a noble cause."

POUDLUM WAS BACK and he had some biscuits with him. He handed us each one and said, "Dese wuz left from breakfast. Thought y'all might be hongry." There was a slice of fried streak-of-lean inside the biscuit. It was mighty tasty. We munched on them until we got to the Mill Creek, then we lay down on our bellies on the bank of the creek and drank from it. When we got up Jake said to me, "I gots to go back up de creek to dat big sweetgum tree where I was gon' meet you. I left my stuff under it."

"All right. Me and Poudlum will sit here on the bank and wait for you."

While we sat dangling our feet in the water Poudlum said, "Won't be long fo' school be starting."

"Yeah, wish there was some way to get out of going."

"Dey ain't. We gots to go."

"Jake said school was good, that I should go a long time."

"Dat's de same thing my momma say. How come we can't go together?"

I didn't know the answer to his question, so I told him so. "I don't know why."

"It's 'cause you is white and I is black, dat's why."

I pondered what he said for a while, then I told him, "That may be the reason, but it don't make no sense."

I heard Jake splashing back down the creek. When he came into view he had his drawstring bag slung over his shoulder. I knew it contained his extra clothes and a few cans of beans and sardines. His old guitar was on his other shoulder and he had two long, slim bamboo poles in his left hand.

I asked, "What you gonna do with them two cane poles? You ain't got no time to fish."

"You is right on dat point, but I figures ifen I sees anybody while I be floating down de creek and across de river, den I gonna pretend dat I's fishing. Any fool know a convict on de run wouldn't be taking time to fish."

Poudlum grinned at me and said, "He be mighty smart."

We all studied the position of the sun, agreed that it was between one and two o'clock, and that it was time to get on down the creek. When we silently crawled into our hiding spot all was quiet across the Saltifa at the still. Six boxes of whiskey were still beneath the table. Old Man Creel hadn't been there yet.

After we had been there for what seemed like about fifteen minutes, Jake whispered, "Why don't we go check out de boat and stash my stuff while we waits?"

We went down the creek bank listening carefully all the while for the sound of the old man's car. When we got there I walked out on the log bridge, straddled it, leaned down, and grabbed the rope and tossed the end of it to Jake.

By the time I got back to the bank they had pulled the boat partially up on the sandy edge of the creek and were surveying the inch of water that stood in it. "Looks like it leaks," Jake said.

I could see the doubt in his eyes, but I knew the boat was sound because it was dry when I found it, and even if it had developed a leak, then it was too small to matter. I told him all this, but he still wasn't convinced.

"Den where de water come from?"

"Water came from the rain."

He said, "Oh, I guess dat makes sense," But I could tell he still wasn't convinced. "Let's all three grab holt of the side, tip it over and pour the water out, then we'll put it back in the water and see what happens."

We accomplished the task, Jake loaded his stuff aboard, stood and said, "Guess dis be my chariot to freedom. Hope it don't sink on me 'cause I can't swim."

"How come you can't swim?"

"Just never learnt how."

"Me neither," Poudlum said.

I knew Jake needed some reassurance. I could see it in his eyes, so I told him, "Jake this is a sound boat. If it wasn't, then it would have already sunk. When you're going down the creek just stay close to the bank if that will make you feel better."

"But when de creek ends I gots to cross de Tombigbee. I hear tell it's a mighty big river."

"It is, but it's just a big muddy lake. Ain't no currents in it. I been swimming in it before. You won't have no trouble paddling right across it."

"But what if, just what if de boat sinks or flips over and I ends up in de water?"

"See that big paddle in the boat?"

"Uh huh."

"It floats. Your guitar will float. All you would have to do is hang on to one or both of them, paddle to the bank and—"

Right then I heard the unmistakable sound of Old Man Cliff Creel's big Fleetmaster station wagon coming down the logging road. "He's coming to get the whiskey! Quick, let's get back!

We heard the engine cut off and then the slamming of the door just as we had secured ourselves back into the hiding place.

In a few moments he emerged from the mouth of the trail. This time he was pushing a wheelbarrow. As usual, he was wearing his hat, but he had shed his Sunday suit coat and loosened his necktie. We watched while he loaded three of the boxes from underneath the table, then he disappeared back down the trail with them. Momentarily he reappeared and repeated the process; except much to my relief, he paused to stuff the fat envelope into the hollow tree before he left with his final load. As soon as the sound of his station wagon's engine faded away I said, "Y'all wait here while I go cross the log bridge and get that envelope."

As soon as I stood up I heard another sound which I instantly recognized. It was the drone of a motor boat coming up the creek, and from having heard it before, I knew how long it would take to get there.

My heart sank as I realized it was the whiskey-maker, with his double-barreled shotgun, coming to get his money out of the tree and I knew I didn't have time to get there before he did.

20

Down the Creek

I knew instantly what I had to do. I didn't like it, but knew that I absolutely could not allow this opportunity to slip away. I had to swim.

"Meet me at the big sweet-gum tree up the Mill Creek," I quickly told Poudlum and Jake.

They didn't move. "It's the whiskey maker—get out of here, now!"

I saw them quickly retreating just before I began a running start toward the deep water of the Satilfa. I dived into the creek as hard as I could and started swimming. It wasn't a dog-paddle either, my past experience of fear of snakes coupled with my present fear of the whiskey-maker caused me to use a strong overhand stroke.

Suddenly I felt my clawing hands and my kicking feet scrub against the sandy bottom. I was across, but I could tell by the sound that the motorboat was just around the bend, only seconds away. My ankles drug through the shallow water, then my feet dug into the bank as I raced toward the money tree. When I reached it I dropped to my knees and frantically dug the debris out of the hole. My fingers closed on the fat envelope, feeling the thickness of it, knowing it meant Jake's freedom, the Robinsons' land and a miracle for my mother. I drug it out of the hollow of the tree, took the extra second to replace the debris, stood up and prepared to run, but it was too late. I heard the bow of the whiskey-maker's boat grinding onto the bank of the creek. The only cover was behind the money tree. I slid behind the trunk of it, sunk to my belly, clutched the envelope tightly and started crawfishing on the floor of the forest. I did this until he cut the engine off and got out of the boat, then the forest became deathly quiet. I had only made it about twelve feet into the forest, settling into a little hollow in the ground, hoping that it wasn't the home of a snake.

I watched while the whiskey-maker grabbed his shotgun, got out of the boat, walked onto the creek bank, and leaned his weapon against a tree. Then he went back to the boat and began unloading his sacks of corn and sugar. I dared not move while he made several trips.

When he had finished stacking his supplies for a new batch of whiskey, he walked over to the money tree and started digging into the hollow. I could see his face. At first he looked puzzled. Then he dug deeper into the hollow. Finally, when he realized there was no money for him, he began to curse Old Man Cliff Creel. He thrashed about the still area uttering curses and obscenities the like of which I had never heard before.

When his vile tirade ended he snatched up his shotgun and started walking down toward his boat. I supposed he was leaving and started to breath a little easier; that is until he got down to the bank and suddenly stopped, bent over and started studying the ground.

When I realized he was looking at my tracks, the terror within me was rekindled. I had left deep prints with my bare feet in the sand when I had come running out of the creek. So deep and plain until I could see them through the leaves myself.

He started walking slowly back up the bank, bent low following my tracks until they disappeared on the dead leaves just before he got to the money tree. Then he stood up straight and looked toward the exact spot where I was hiding.

I began to consider my options: Get up and run, but, no, that lean, mean man would run me down in no time. Make me a dash for the creek and swim for it. That seemed like the best choice. Maybe he couldn't swim. I knew he couldn't swim fast with his overalls and brogans on, but then there was that shot gun in his hands.

He took a tentative step toward where I was hidden, leaned over and looked intently in my direction. I longed for the sweet sound of Jake's slingshot, but I knew that was too much to hope for. I also knew he couldn't see me yet, but a few more steps and he would be able to.

I decided on the creek. I figured I could beat him to the bank, dive in and go underwater immediately, then swim as far as I could underneath the surface. Maybe I could stay under all the way across.

I tensed my whole body and prepared to spring up from my prone position, then suddenly, from the woods across the creek came these crashing sounds as if a bear was thrashing around over there.

The whiskey-maker jerked around to face in that direction, lifting the shotgun to his shoulder. Then, just as quickly there was once again dead silence. He continued looking across the creek, then just about jumped out of his overalls when the same sounds started coming from the woods up the creek toward the fallen tree bridge.

He and his shotgun turned in that direction while he started walking sideways toward his boat. I could tell he was scared. He was looking all about, holding the shotgun ready at his hip while he retreated down the bank.

The crashing sounds from up the creek ceased, but then, moments later a loud splashing sound occurred when something hit the water up there.

That did the trick. The whiskey-maker ran to his boat, pushed it off the bank, leapt aboard, started his motor, turned the craft down stream and left a large wake in the water as he raced away.

I crawled out of my hole, got to my feet and walked out into the open area of the still, wondering what had really happened.

I was standing there, damp and itching, when Poudlum appeared on the bank of the creek across from me and shouted across, "Is you all right?"

Before I could answer Jake called out from up the creek, "Come on up to where de boat is."

I waved at Poudlum and pointed up in that direction, then I walked numbly up that way. They were both waiting for me on my side of the creek when I got there. I could tell they were concerned when Jake said, "Ain't no way we wuz gonna leave you by yo' self."

"What was all that racket?" I asked weakly.

Jake said, "Me and Poudlum saw what wuz happening so we decided what we wuz gonna do, den we split up, picked up a dead limb and started beating de bushes wid it. Den I threw a big dead log into de creek. Dat's when dat man wid de shotgun run off. I had my slingshot ready if he hadn't."

"Y'all did real good. Thank you both. Let's cross the log bridge and see what's in this envelope."

I FELT DRAINED and just wanted to end the escapade. We got across the log bridge, all sat down on the ground and I ripped the thick envelope open. More money than any of us could imagine spilled out on the ground between us. We sat there for a few moments just staring at it. "You can count it, Jake," I said. I was too exhausted.

I watched while he stacked the singles, fives, tens, and twenties into separate stacks.

"Lawd have mercy," Jake said. "Dis is mo money dan I ever seed in my life."

"How much is it?" I asked. "It's got to be a lot because there was six boxes with forty-eight bottles in each one."

"Dey is $576 here. Mr. Creel wuz paying two dollars a bottle, I figures."

"How much is that each if we split it three ways?"

He took a while to decipher and put the money into three different stacks. When he finished he said, "It come to $192 each—a heap of money."

"Good," I said. "That's enough to get you to California, enough for the Robinsons to pay their property taxes, and more. Then, there's more than enough for my mother to pay for what she needs."

Money always breeds problems.

"Where I gonna say I got dis money from?" Poudlum asked.

Jake had all the answers. He said, "Poudlum, you just put dat money in yo' momma's flour barrel. She gon' know what to do wid it when she finds it. And you, Mister Ted, you does de same. Den, tomorrow morning, when y'alls mommas get up to make biscuits dey gon' find de money and do what needs to be done wid it. And ain't none of us gon' ever mention dis day again."

We all promised and the next thing Jake said was mighty sad sounding to my ears. "It be time fo' me to be gitting on down de creek, little fellows."

Poudlum and I watched while he tucked his share of the money away and untied his boat. Before he got into it we both grabbed him around the waist and hugged him. He patted us each on the head and said, "Y'all both gon' grow up to be fine righteous young mens, now turn me loose and let me get gone."

We stepped back and watched him get into the boat, then we reluctantly pushed it off the bank and into the water.

I wasn't crying out loud, but I could feel and taste the hot salty tears running down my face as I watched him right the boat with the paddle and move to the center of the creek.

Just before he disappeared underneath the tree bridge he called out, "I gon' write y'all a letter from California."

I called back, "Don't put no return address on the envelope."

The last thing I ever heard Jake say was, "You sho is a smart white boy." Then he was gone.

POUDLUM AND I stood there a few moments. We were glad and we were sad. Glad that Jake was going free, but sad that he was leaving us. When the sound of Jake's paddle bumping against the side of the boat finally faded away, Poudlum and I turned and walked through the woods toward the Mill Creek. When we got there we looped our arms over each other's shoulders and started walking up the small stream. We didn't talk, we just walked.

When we reached the place where we would have exited the creek to go toward the Robinsons' burned-out cotton house, we stopped and began to talk. I said, "Poudlum, we done got the money and we done seen that Jake got away. There's just one more thing I want to see."

"What's dat?"

I want to see Old Man Cliff Creel get caught with his load of whiskey. You want to come?"

"What time does you think it is?"

"'Bout two or two thirty."

"I 'spect my momma and 'em probably looking fo' me by now."

"Yeah, mine too."

"Probably gon' get a whupping when I does get home."

"Yeah, me too."

"We don't have to get close enough so dat we has to deal wid dat dog, does we?"

"No, we'll watch from across the road."

"You hungry?"

"Yeah, I'm real hongry."

"Let's go on up the creek to the big sweet gum tree, then go up through the woods, past the sawmill to the store."

"You think de sto be open?"

"Yeah, Miss Lena usually opens about one o'clock on Sunday after church. Let's go get us an ice cream sandwich and a Nehi."

"Ice cream sandwich costs a dime."

An ice cream sandwich was a special treat because it was so good and cost so much, but today was a special day and we surely had the funds, so I told Poudlum, "We got plenty of money. In fact, I think we ought to each keep ourselves five dollars and eat ice cream sandwiches the rest of the summer."

"Let's keep ten and eat 'em all next summer, too," he grinned.

There was an eeriness about the sawmill when we passed through it. I wanted to tell Poudlum about the sawdust pile and how much fun it was to slide down it, but it just didn't seem like the place I had always been so infatuated by. The pile of logs was down to just a few dozen and there were only a few stacks of fresh-sawn lumber. At Jake's shack, where he would have had a hot bed of coals to heat his coffee, there were only cold, gray ashes. It was as if the place was slowly dying.

I quickened my step and said, "Come on, Poudlum, let's hurry."

"Hey, ain't dat yo' brother, Fred, up at de sto?"

Sure enough, Fred was sitting on the ground, his back to an oak tree, nursing a Nehi. When we got close he looked up at Poudlum and said, "Hey, Poudlum."

Then he turned his head toward me and asked, "Your belly feeling better?"

"Yeah. I'll be right back. Poudlum, just wait here."

Miss Lena was busy with a customer and didn't have time to talk. She just took my dollar, smiled, and gave me my change. Back outside, I handed Poudlum a drink, and him and Fred both an ice cream sandwich.

Fred took his, looked startled and said, "You just spent most of what you made yesterday."

"I been saving," I said. "How was church today?"

"Wasn't no church."

"Huh?"

"Well it got started, but it didn't last long."

"What happened?"

"After all the singing and praying, Brother Benny started his usual crazy jabbering, but I knew right off that something was wrong when he fell off the pulpit."

"What in the world caused him to do that?"

"He was drunk."

"He was drunk in church? How you know that?"

"'Cause he landed right on his face and busted a bottle of whiskey he had in his coat pocket. You could smell it all over the church."

The first time I could remember missing church and all

this had to happen today. I sure was sorry I had missed it and couldn't wait to hear more. "What did everybody do?"

"Nothing at first. He was out cold. Everybody just sat there until that whiskey smell started spreading, then Aunt Cleo yelled out from the front pew, 'My God, the man's drunk!'"

"And then?"

"Everybody got up and went outside. When I was leaving they was having a meeting around the dinner tables."

"What happened to the preacher?"

"Last thing I saw was Old Man Cliff Creel loading him into his station wagon."

Hearing that old man's name reminded me why we were here. "How long you been here?"

"'Bout half an hour. I left mother at Uncle Curtis's and went home, but Daddy and Ned hadn't come back out of the woods, so I ate some leftover breakfast then walked over here."

"You ain't seen him ride by here, have you?"

"Who?"

"Old Man Cliff Creel."

"Naw, but that's the third time I've seen that car there go by."

I looked up and saw a large black four-door car. It was moving slow and I could see two men inside it, both wearing hats, white shirts, and neckties.

"That's a brand-new 1948 Hudson Commodore," Fred said.

It was coming from towards Coffeeville.

When the car passed us it turned left onto Friendship

Road so that the rear of it was towards us.

"See that license plate? That car is from Montgomery County and it says it's a state government vehicle. I wonder who they are and what they're doing down here."

I looked over toward Poudlum. He was already on his feet. We both knew who they were.

21

The Miracle

Just a few seconds after the state agent's car disappeared, Old Man Cliff Creel's station wagon topped the hill heading west toward his house.

"Hey, where y'all going?" Fred called out, but we were already running down the road and didn't stop to answer him.

We were about halfway to the old man's house when the big black Hudson passed us. We had to move off the road and walk in the ditch to avoid the swirling tunnel of dust the car left behind.

"We gon' miss de fireworks," Poudlum said.

"Yeah, I know. We should have waited on those ice cream sandwiches and gone straight to the woods across from the old man's house."

"What you thinks dey gonna do wid 'im?

"I don't know. Haul him off to jail I reckon."

"Who gonna feed and water his cows?"

"Shoot, I don't know, Poudlum. I suppose he's got some

family nearby who'll get word of it and come take care of 'em."

"What ifen he ain't?"

"Ain't what?"

"Got no family hereabouts?"

"Don't worry. By tomorrow everybody will know about it and somebody'll take care of 'em."

The dust had settled and we moved back onto the road and resumed a brisk jog when I heard Fred yell from behind us, "Hey, y'all wait up."

We slowed a little and before Fred was within hearing Poudlum said, "Might as well tell him, 'cause like you says, everybody gonna know about it tomorrow."

"Okay, we'll tell him everything, except nothing about Jake or the money."

"Course not. We promised on dat."

"Promised what?" Fred asked through heavy breathing as he caught up.

"Uh—that we were gonna be at Old Man Cliff Creel's to see this happen."

"See what happen? Y'all better tell me what the heck's going on."

"I will, but let's keep running. You know that car you said had a state government tag on it?"

"Yeah, it came back out from Friendship Road and headed this way right after y'all took off."

"We think they are from the—" I struggled to remember what Jake had called them. "I think they're the Alabama Alcohol something."

"Whiskey Police," Poudlum said.

"Well, if they are, what makes y'all think they're going to Old Man Cliff Creel's house?"

"'Cause he's got a load of bootleg whiskey in his station wagon."

"Naw, he ain't got no such thing!" Fred said in disbelief.

"Does too," Poudlum said. "We seed him load it up."

Between breaths, still jogging, Fred exclaimed, "If what y'all are saying is true, then Old Man Cliff Creel is the bootlegger."

"Dat's right," Poudlum said. "And dey is fixing to take him away."

Poudlum was right. We were too late for the fireworks. When the house came into sight we saw the men in white shirts and ties escorting the old man into the back seat of the big Hudson. He didn't look happy, and there I went again, feeling sorry for someone who didn't deserve my sympathy. While we watched the big car drive away towards Coffeeville, Fred declared, "Well I'll be, they had handcuffs on him."

We all three just stood there in the road for a while. Poudlum finally broke the silence when he said, "We probably oughts to close dat gate so de rest of dem cows won't get out."

"What gate?" Fred asked.

I pointed down the fence line across the road and said, "Down there, where we stole Poudlum's cow this morning."

"Y'all stole a cow?"

"A chicken, too," Poudlum said.

"What in the world is he talking about?" Fred asked.

I motioned for them to follow and started walking across the road. They quickly caught up with me and I said, "We sneaked Poudlum's cow out while everybody was at church this morning. We didn't have time to get the gate closed 'cause that big bulldog came after us."

Fred stopped in his tracks and exclaimed, "I know that dog! It's a wonder y'all got away without being mauled."

"'Bout didn't get away," Poudlum said.

"What happened?" Fred asked him.

Poudlum pointed off to our right and said, "He chased us up dat big pine over yonder. Kept us treed for a good while; dat's until he got his bad self popped in de nuts by a rock from a slingshot, den he finally went on off."

Fred turned to me and said, "Good shot!"

I looked at Poudlum and he mutely looked back at me. I didn't want to take undue credit, but on the other hand, I couldn't tell that Jake had fired the shot, so I mumbled, "Thanks," and kept walking.

We were almost to the gate. "What if dat dog done got back to being his nasty, mean self?" Poudlum asked.

Fred extended his hand toward me and said, "Give me your stick. That dog's been chasing me for years. I'll bust his head if he so much as sticks it around that gatepost."

When I handed it over he said, "Now, y'all go ahead and close the gate."

Poudlum and I lifted and pushed, then I slid the latch and it was done. There was no sound or sight of the dog.

We walked with Poudlum to the road leading toward his house, where just before we said good-bye he said, "Mr. Curvin probably gon' be taking de last of our cotton to de gin come Tuesday. Does you wants to go?"

"Yeah. If I don't see him before, tell him to pick me up at Miss Lena's."

While we walked home Fred listened intently after I promised to tell him everything; that is, everything except what I had already promised not to tell. I was careful not to mention Jake and the money. When I finished I thought I had done a real good job, but I hadn't thought about one thing.

"Wait a minute," Fred said, "how come you and Poudlum knew who those men in the new Hudson was, and why they were here?"

"Well, I can tell you about that," I said. But I couldn't. I was just stalling for time until I could think of something. I didn't like not telling my brother the truth, but it was for the best. It came to me, but I hated the thought of using someone who had been generous and kind to me; however she was gone and I had no other choice.

"It was Mrs. Blossom."

"Huh?"

"Yeah, I think she knew about the old man and wrote a letter to the state people in Montgomery."

"How in the world would she know?"

I was saved from any further lying by the rattling of Uncle Curvin's truck coming up behind us. He slowed to a crawl and stuck his toothless head out the window. "Y'all jump on and I'll give you a ride home."

Just before we turned off Friendship Road towards our house we met my cousin Robert on his way back home after dropping my mother off. He stopped beside us and said, "Hey, Uncle Curvin, you hear about the preacher being drunk today?"

Uncle Curvin wasn't much of a churchgoer either.

"Yeah, I heard. Shore do wish I had been there."

"Where you coming from?" Robert asked.

"Coffeeville."

"Anything going on there!"

I was straddling the side of the truck and could see Uncle Curvin's gums when he grinned and said, "Saw a couple of fellas from the state beverage control gassing up their car."

"What they doing round here?"

"They had Old Man Cliff Creel handcuffed in the back seat."

"What—how come?"

"Beats me."

"Did you talk to him?"

"Naw, but I did talk to the fella driving the car."

"What did he say?"

"Said the old man wanted me to take care of his livestock till he gets back."

"I wonder why—"

Fred chimed in. "I know why they got 'im, 'cause he's the bootlegger, that's why."

Robert and Uncle Curvin both looked towards us on the back of the truck, staring in disbelief. After a moment Robert asked, "How you know something like that?"

"'Cause we was walking by his house, me, Ted, and Poudlum. We seen 'em when they put him in the back of their car."

"That don't mean he's the bootlegger," Robert said.

All eyes turned to me when Fred said, "He is though. You tell 'em, Ted."

I was kicking Fred with the foot I had inside the truck body because I didn't want everybody else to know everything I knew. I knew I could trust Uncle Curvin, but I also knew cousin Robert would be taking the news on down the road and that within two days it would be common knowledge within ten square miles. However, I knew I had to tell something now that Fred had implicated me, so I told them about the two times I had spied on him: the time I saw him and the preacher drinking whiskey in his back yard and the time I saw him transferring the boxes of whiskey from his station wagon to his smokehouse, using the excuse that I was taking a short cut through the woods.

When I finished Robert said, "But you don't know it was whiskey in those boxes."

"I saw him pull a bottle of whiskey out of a box and give it to Brother Benny. That box was just like all the others."

That was enough for Robert. He shoved the truck into gear and said, "I got to go tell Daddy. See y'all later."

I knew Uncle Curvin couldn't hear me as we rumbled on towards our house.

"Fred—"

"I know, I shouldn't have said nothing."

"Promise me you won't never tell about me and Poudlum ever knowing about or being at that still. What if Old Man Cliff Creel busted out of prison and found out. He would probably think we told on him. Now, you promise."

"All right, I won't never tell nobody."

Uncle Curvin lingered in the yard with me when we got home. Fred immediately took off for the back yard where we could see daddy and Ned dressing a turkey.

"You think my cotton house is empty? I'll be gathering my corn crop pretty soon and be needing a place to store it."

"Yes sir, I believe it's empty as of today. If anybody had been in it, then they probably would be floating down the Satilfa right now planning to cross the Tombigbee at first dark. If you drive over the bridge early tomorrow morning you could probably find yourself a good boat laying around the bank somewhere."

Uncle Curvin started snickering, then he said, "Miss Lena told me what that sorry polecat of a sheriff said to you."

"You think he'll bother us anymore?"

"Nope. I think he's got bigger things to worry about now, what with the old man being arrested. Looks like J. D. got himself a turkey. 'Spect I might just stay for supper. I can eat the dressing and the gravy."

I found that big gobbler's long black beard lying across the latch to our bedroom door. I would let it dry out a few days before adding it to my collection in the cigar box.

Before long the wonderful aroma of roast turkey was drifting through the house. That night, when we were all gathered around the table enjoying the meal, my mother couldn't stop talking about the preacher being drunk at church and my father couldn't stop laughing about it.

"It's not funny, J. D.," she said. "And I can tell you this—he won't be back. The congregation had a meeting outside the church and the deacons voted to fire him. Now we got to find us a new preacher. I can't get over it, a preacher, drunk in church trying to deliver a sermon!"

Well, she got over it real quick when Uncle Curvin told the news about Old Man Cliff Creel. It was just too much for one day. I thought she was going to faint. For some reason it didn't seem to surprise my father.

Uncle Curvin promised to pick me up Tuesday morning and I went to sleep listening to the grownups' voices drone on and on about the events of the day.

Sometime during the middle of the night I woke up and remembered that all that money was still in the pocket of my jeans, lying on the floor. I picked them up after I slid out of bed and made sure my brothers were sound asleep, then I slipped them on and went out of the open window. Outside, the sky was lit up by the moon and a million bright stars so that I had no trouble seeing to skim off my nine dollars and some change. I quickly scooted underneath the house and deposited it in my jar, then I walked around the house to the back door leading into the kitchen. I was thankful to see it was slightly open, just enough so that I could slide through without making a noise. I tiptoed across the floor until I was exactly where I knew my mother's big wooden bowl was, the one where she kept her flour for biscuit making. I gently lifted the lid, deposited $182 in the center of the bowl, and raked a handful of flour over the pile of money.

I was halfway out of the room when I reached out towards the kitchen table to steady myself. My hand hit the globe of the kerosene lamp, knocking it off its base. It hit the floor, shattering itself and the silence.

My first instinct was to run, but then I thought about my bare feet and all the sharp pieces of glass on the floor; also I didn't want to cause any further fright to my parents, so I just froze.

"Who's in there!" Mother shouted.

"It's me, Mother. It's okay," I weakly responded.

I heard the sound as she scraped the tip of a big wooden match across the side of the match box, then I saw the glow of the lamp after she lit it. When she appeared at the door I said, "Wait, there's glass all over the floor."

She bent over, placed the lamp on the floor and said, "Don't move, I'll be right back."

She was back in a moment with a quilt which she folded double, then furled it out so that it reached from the door to my feet. "Now, walk across the quilt on in here."

When I reached her she hugged me and asked, "What in the world are you doing up rambling around this time of night?"

I was over the shock and had had time to think. "Uh, I don't know. I just woke up in the kitchen."

My father was awake by now. "What's going on?" he asked.

"Lord have mercy," she said. "This child has been walking in his sleep. Come on, you're sleeping with us the rest of the night. I'll sweep that mess up in the morning."

I woke up after daylight not knowing where I was, then I realized I was in my parents' bed, alone. The first sound I heard was my mother stirring about in the kitchen while she sung a hymn. The first thing I saw was the flour on my hand.

I leapt out of bed, quickly slipped my jeans on and went to the front porch to wash up. When I got to the kitchen I asked, "Where's daddy?"

"He left before daylight. S. T. Brooks came and picked him up. They gone to Mobile to look for work. Your brothers are still asleep. Did you wash up?"

"Yes, ma'am."

"Then sit down. Biscuits will be out of the oven in a minute."

When I was seated at the table she asked, "Son, do you believe in miracles?"

"Yes, ma'am."

"You sure?"

"Uh huh."

"Well, if the Lord granted you a miracle, would you tell other folks about it or would you just keep it between you and the Lord?"

"I believe I would just keep it between me and the Lord and go on about my business."

"That's what I think too, and that's what I'll do. Here's you a hot biscuit and some of your brother Ned's honey to go on it."

My brother robbed honey trees. Me, I robbed money trees.

22

A Yellow Watermelon

Poudlum and I were flat on our backs looking up at a clear blue sky from a bed of fluffy white cotton, on the way to the gin. His mother and father were in the cab with Uncle Curvin.

"You bring some money wid you?" Poudlum asked.

"Yeah, I got a dollar and sixty cents. You?"

"Uh huh, I gots me two dollars. We be going into Grove Hill after we leaves de gin. My momma and daddy gon' go to de court house to pay de taxes. While dey doing dat, maybe we can find us some stuff to buy."

"Fred told me they got a drug store there where you can buy funny books and ice cream. We'll go there first."

"Sound good to me. What yo' momma say about de money?"

"She didn't say nothing. Yours?"

"Naw, she never mentioned it, but she shore wuz happy when she wuz making biscuits yesterday morning."

"What did she say about your cow being back?"

"At first she was worried about what Old Man Cliff Creel would do; dat is until I told her what happened to him, den she got her pail and starting milking."

There were only two trucks in front of us at the gin, since cotton picking time was winding down. We got off the truck and marveled at the big tube as it sucked every fiber of cotton off the back of the truck. I was glad. I didn't want to see any more cotton for a while. After the Robinsons collected their money Poudlum and I got back on the truck. The ride into town was short. Our first stop was at the post office. We all waited while Uncle Curvin went inside to buy a money order for our school clothes. My mother had given him the order, the money, and the instructions early this morning. I remembered her telling my uncle, "Now, don't you forget, Curvin. We barely got enough time to get 'em here before these young 'uns got to start back to school."

After my uncle completed his task we drove down the street to a stop sign, turned left and there was the county courthouse sitting right in the middle of the street. It was the biggest structure I had ever seen with big gray pillars across the front, all of them as big as any log I had ever seen at the sawmill. It looked ominous to me and I didn't want to go near it, but I was curious about the monument we parked next to. As soon as we got out of the truck I asked Uncle Curvin about it. "It was put there to honor the dead soldiers of the Confederate army. You see that cement bench next to it?"

"Yes, sir."

"That's where I want you sitting when I get back."

"Dat goes for you too, Poudlum," Mrs. Robinson said

just before she and Mr. Robinson turned and began walking toward the courthouse.

"Where you going?" I asked my uncle.

"I'm going to Horton's grocery store to fill this list your mother gave me. It's about halfway up the street on the left." He pointed in the direction of the store and asked, "You see it over yonder?"

"Yes, sir."

"That's where I'll be."

"We wanna go to the drug store."

"I reckon that'll be all right. It's up there on the right side of the street just before you get to the corner. Y'all got some money?"

"Yes, sir."

"All right, y'all behave yourselves and I'll see y'all right here, on this bench."

"Yes, sir. Come on, Poudlum."

We crossed the street and got on the sidewalk where we passed another grocery store called the Piggly Wiggly. It had a sign over the door of a fat cartoon-looking pink pig.

"Dis place a lot bigger dan Coffeeville," Poudlum said.

"Yeah."

Next we passed a furniture store, a hardware store, then there it was, Chapman's Drug Store. We stared through the big glass windows for a while. We could see a rack full of comic books, a round tower with sacks of candy hanging on it and a long white marble counter with black stools supported by shining medal pedestals in front of it. We watched while two teenage girls went in, sat on two of the stools and started talking to a man behind the counter. He turned and set pewter dishes in front of them filled with ice cream covered with syrup and fruit. I had had ice cream before, but never like that. The girls began to eat with tiny round spoons.

I looked at Poudlum and his eyes were as big as mine. "Come on," I said, "We're going in there. Let's look at the funny books first."

Fred had a stack of comic books, but none were new and shiny like these. While we were trying to decide on a selection I noticed three ladies who walked up to the counter and asked the man behind it for ice cream cones.

"What flavor, ladies? We got vanilla, strawberry, and chocolate."

When they got their cones they turned and walked out with them instead of sitting down.

Poudlum was poking me with one hand while he held two comic books in the other. "Let's get dese two Captain Marvels. Dey different. When we finishes dem we can trade."

"All right. Let's get two sacks of candy and take some home to everybody else."

We took the comic books and two sacks of jawbreakers over and laid them on the marble counter next to the man's cash register.

He looked at us over the tope of his glasses, didn't smile or say hello. "That'll be thirty cents."

I started climbing on one of the stools and said, "We want some ice cream too, sir. In those dishes with the little spoons." I patted the stool next to me and said, "Climb up here next to me, Poudlum."

That man came out from behind the counter like the place was on fire. He grabbed my arm and said, "You take your little friend and get on out of here."

I was shocked, but not speechless. "What for? We ain't done nothing."

He froze for a moment, then he leaned down and with his face two inches from mine he said, "Don't you know, young man, that we don't serve colored folks in here. Now, y'all get gone from here."

He opened the big glass door, pushed Poudlum and I out onto the sidewalk, then closed it behind him. We just stood there for a moment until I realized we didn't even have our comic books and candy. "Wait here, Poudlum."

I walked back inside, went up to the counter, placed forty cents on it next to our purchases and said, "This is for the funny books and the candy. I want two ice cream cones, too."

"What flavor?" he asked with an icy voice.

"Chocolate, please."

When I got back outside and presented Poudlum with his ice cream cone he looked at it and said, "Don't know why dey don't serve colored folks. Dey serves colored ice cream." Then he licked it and said, "Good, too."

We were sitting on the concrete bench under the shadow cast by the statue of the Confederate soldier eating our ice cream cones watching cars and trucks go by. After a while I noticed that the people in every single one stared at me and Poudlum as they went by.

"I don't know why everybody keeps looking at us when they go by," I said between licks.

"I knows why," Poudlum said.

"You do?"

"Uh huh."

"Why?"

"'Cause dey ain't use to seeing a white boy and a colored boy being together, specially sitting here underneath dis monument."

"Well, they can just get use to it, 'cause ain't nothing wrong with it. And someday you gonna be able to walk in that drug store, sit down and have yourself some ice cream. You know what else, one day we'll be able to go to school together, too."

"Huh? How you know all dat?"

"'Cause I know what's right, I can feel it."

"Oh yeah? It may be right, but who gon' make all dis happen?"

"If it's necessary, you and me. We ain't gonna be young 'uns forever."

"How in de world is we gon' change de way people thinks, when we gets big?"

"We'll teach 'em, but sometimes we may have to do what my daddy told me."

"What's dat?"

"Carry us a big stick."

IT WAS SATURDAY, a week and four days since I had seen Poudlum, and only one more week before school started. All the school clothes had come. The mail rider had left all the packages at Miss Lena's store yesterday. Uncle Curvin had picked them up and brought them to our house. My brothers and I tried them all on and our mother cried while telling us how handsome we looked. My father hadn't come back from Mobile yet. He sent some money and word that he was working.

It was about two hours before dark when Mrs. Robinson and Poudlum showed up at our house. She brought a big bunch of turnip greens with huge purple and white roots on them. Poudlum had a big striped watermelon on his shoulder.

While our Mothers sat on the front porch talking about the best ways to cook your greens, Poudlum tugged at my sleeve and said, "Come on out in de yard."

Once we were out of hearing from our mothers Poudlum asked, "Where yo' brothers?"

"Ned's gone to see his girlfriend, Betty Lynn Findley, and Fred left with Uncle Curvin, going somewhere."

"So ain't nobody around but us?"

"That right. Why?"

"'Cause we got a letter from Jake and dere's a note in it fo' you."

"Where is it?"

"I gots it here in de bib of my overalls."

Poudlum pulled the piece of paper out and I snatched it from his fingers and began to read:

Mister Ted,

    Thanks to you, I made it all the way to California. I got some work too. Out here they likes my music and pays me to play and sing. You knows what else, out here I is a Negro man and not a nigger. Remember, go to school and learn, cause knowledge be power.

Jake

"Can I keep this, Poudlum?"

"Course you can. It be to you from Jake. Come on, let's go back up to de porch. Looks like our mommas getting ready to cut dat melon. It be a special melon, too."

"How's it special?"

"You waits and see."

My mother was standing in the yard at the edge of the porch with her big butcher knife facing the ripe melon in front of her. When she cut into it, it made a popping sound like it just couldn't wait to burst open.

When the two halves fell apart, I was stunned to see that instead of being red inside, it was yellow. "Why, that melon is yellow," I exclaimed.

"Dat melon is like people—it may be a different color, but it still be a watermelon," Poudlum announced, as if to the world.

I accepted a slice, felt the juicy, sweet crunch of it in my mouth when I bit into it, and with the juice dripping from my chin I said, "It's sweet as sugar, too, just like a red one."

Check out these other titles from **Junebug Books**

LONGLEAF
ROGER REID

Jason and his forest-smart friend Leah must survive
a harrowing night lost in Alabama's Conecuh National Forest.

JB

CRACKER'S MULE
BILLY MOORE

A boy spending a summer in 1950s Alabama
suffers ridicule as he raises a blind mule.

JB

LITTLE BROTHER REAL SNAKE
BILLY MOORE

The son of a brave Plains warrior overcomes challenges
on a quest to take his place in his tribe.

JB

THE CREEK CAPTIVES
HELEN BLACKSHEAR

This pulse-pounding collection tells stories of when the South
was our new nation's "wild west," based on true events.

JB

THE GOLD DISC OF COOSA
VIRGINIA POUNDS BROWN

A narration of the historic meeting between
the explorer DeSoto and the last of the Alabama Moundbuilders.

Read chapters, purchase books, and learn more at
WWW.NEWSOUTHBOOKS.COM/JUNEBUG